Great Australian Legends

Great Australian Legends

Frank Hardy
(in association with Truthful Jones)
Story consultant Anne Turnbull

Illustrated by Alan Moir

HUTCHINSON AUSTRALIA

Century Hutchinson Australia Pty Ltd
89-91 Albion Street, Surry Hills, New South Wales 2010

Sydney   Melbourne   London
Auckland   Johannesburg
and agencies throughout the world

First published 1988

Reprinted 1989

National Library of Australia
Cataloguing-in-Publication Data

Hardy, Frank, 1917– .
   Great Australian legends.

   ISBN 0 09 169141 9.

   I. Moir, Alan, 1947– . II. Title.
A823'.3

Designed by Helen Semmler
Typeset in Baskerville by Bookset Pty Ltd
Printed by The Book Printer, Maryborough, Victoria

Contents

Preface   1

1   *That* Aboriginal myths are part of Australian folklore.   9

2   *That* Australians would complain in heaven.   12

3   *That* many Australians have had a leg bitten
off by a crocodile.   16

4   *That* you can't judge people by the clothes
they wear.   21

5   *That* money doesn't make much difference.   25

6   *That* some of the wealth of millionaires
seeps down to the poor.   29

7   *That* the Aborigines acted in self-defence
when killing white man's cattle.   33

8   *That* Australian men are great lovers.   37

9   *That* Australian women always have the last word.   41

10   *That* Australia is the lucky country but
Australians are the unluckiest people in the world.   46

11   *That* the Aussie battler is better known
than the Pope.   51

12   *That* there are more eccentrics in Australia
than anywhere else on earth.   55

13   *That* the friend of today is the enemy of tomorrow.   62

14   *That* Australians are the world's worst worriers.   65

15 *That* Australians will not admit to being illiterate. 68

16 *That* Australia has the highest beer consumption rate in the world. 73

17 *That* vomiting is an art. 78

18 *That* Australian men have big dongers. 86

19 *That* Aborigines have a different attitude to democracy. 90

20 *That* greed and revenge are a terrible mixture. 94

21 *That* cheats never prosper—if they've got principles. 101

22 *That* punishment is not the way to stop crime. 107

23 *That* They won't give a battler a fair go. 112

24 *That* the Melbourne—Sydney argument can be settled. 115

25 *That* every battler could be a virtuoso— given the chance. 119

26 *That* Australians value dogs more than people. 124

27 *That* when you want work you can't find it and when you don't everyone offers you a job. 129

28 *That* Darwinism was used to justify white racism. 133

29 *That* the hunger for knowledge is more powerful than advertising. 138

30 *That* Australians always want to be somewhere else. 141

31 *That* you can't win on the racetrack— even when you pick the card. 146

32 *That* workers' compensation is a God-given right. 153

33 *That* you should never take advice from a barber. 157

34 *That* Australians love to be praised. 162

35 *That* cricket, like grand opera, is funny because it is so deadly earnest. 166

36 *That* the Jolly Swagman was the most Australian Australian. 170

37 *That* the halt, the lame and the dead vote early and often in Australian politics 176

Preface

Legends are created and people live by them; this has happened in every country on earth.

In legend is robed the will of the people.

The Australian continent is rich in legends and myths. The myths of the Aboriginal people go back thousands of years; those of the white settlers, 200 years.

Most of the legends in this book have been created by the white settlers. A few deal with the clash of cultures, with the impact of European occupation on Aboriginal life and society. Differing attitudes to capital punishment are revealed in the myth of Musquito, the only known Aboriginal bushranger; to the ownership of land and cattle in the Gurindji myth of Burunjuk's encounter with white men and their animals; to the concept of democracy in the tale about the first Aboriginal voters; to the justification of 'arsenic in the damper' mass murder by the influence of Darwin's theory of the 'survival of the fittest'.

The myths of the Aborigines are safe in the hands of the tribal songmen (or story-tellers) and are being recorded by white historians and anthropologists and, more recently and

1

importantly, by the Aborigines themselves.

At a luncheon to launch the bicentennial project '200 Untold Stories' I proposed that, as well as gathering 'true' stories, an attempt should be made to collect the myths by which we have lived. Interest was expressed and Geraldine Doogue interviewed me on the radio about the idea; but nothing was done about it.

So I decided to write this book.

I felt that amongst the hundreds of yarns I'd collected and refined or (more often) made up might run the thread of the myths and legends by which the ordinary Australian, significantly known as the Aussie battler, had lived and which are reflected in present-day values and attitudes. I found more than thirty which fulfil this definition, however obliquely. Then, by a simple device of defining the myth illustrated, I fitted together the picture in the Australian jigsaw puzzle. The majority of the legends already existed in the archives of my oral and written yarns; only a few were written after the book was conceived, to supply the missing pieces.

Legends are always created by the common people but, when myth cuts across the aims of the ruling class, attempts are made to rewrite the legends, even to rewrite history; and to introduce new myths which cut across traditional legend-based ideals. Recent years in Australia have seen extreme examples of this rewriting of history or, rather, remythologising of legend-based attitudes.

Australian folk humour has been based on an amused acceptance that the terms of life are those of defeat, that 'you can't win' in life's poker game because the cards are stacked against you; and you can't beat the system because wealth and power are on its side.

'You can't win—but you've got to battle.' This definition of the basis of Australian humour arose from a discussion with artist Vane Lindesay when he was illustrating my first book of Australian yarns, *The Yarns of Billy Borker*, twenty-five years ago. I called a recent book of short stories *The Loser Now Will Be Later to Win*. The title is a line from a Bob Dylan song; he could not have known that his concept was already enshrined in the legends of a whole nation.

The struggle against adversity has lain at the heart of Australian humour, and in the choice of heroes enshrined in folklore. The legend of Ned Kelly has been under attack but, call him failed cattle thief (as Paul Hogan did), thug or murderer, still the greatest praise you can lavish on an Australian is to say he is as game as Ned Kelly. Ned Kelly was a bushranger, but he also stood for the small settlers against powerful landed interests; he lost but he fought hard and died game.

Apart from yarns or legends reflecting the early clashes between Aboriginal culture and that of the white settlers, the first yarn that is unquestionably Australian and not drawn from other cultures, as folk-tales sometimes are, is called 'The Great Australian Whinger' or 'How Would I Be?' It has been around for more than a hundred years, in one form or another. It will, but should not, come as a surprise to many Australians that their most identifiable yarn should be about a whinger who complained in heaven. We are fond of telling yarns about whinging Poms and this yarn reflects the abiding fact that our forebears were the original whinging Poms, the convicts, and that our present-day attitudes towards authority began amongst them (and, of course, the Irish convicts).

For the first convicts escape was difficult, revolt impossible; so they whinged and complained in tale and ballad but always behind the backs of their tormentors. They whinged and found cunning ways of fiddling around the rules and laws.

Australia has more laws that are broken more often than any other country on earth, more regulations that are ignored, more political authorities that are held in contempt, more ways of diddling the government. And more ways to rebel but always, like the convicts of old, short of revolution. It is said that Australia has suffered from the lack of a revolution, and this is true if you don't count the Eureka rebellion or the insurrections of shearers in Queensland in 1891 (though evidence is now emerging that our history has been rewritten to hide the fact that the latter were part of an abortive Communist/anarchist revolt).

Cheating authority, fiddling around the rules and setting up 'stings', are the most prevalent themes in Australian

mythical yarns. This surprised me and the above is the only explanation I can find to it (and remember, I discovered the legends in the yarns, rather than imposed them on the yarns).

Only one yarn of the racetracks is included here, 'The World's Worst Urger'; but dozens exist, many about stings (often unsuccessful—even the racetrack trickster knows he can't win but, of course, he continues to battle to beat the odds).

Australian yarn-spinners are ever ready to dispense advice and home-grown philosophy: 'Never take advice from a barber', 'Punishment is not the way to stop crime', 'Workers' compensation is a God-given right', 'Democracy has to work both ways', 'Money doesn't make much difference', 'Horse-racing is a lottery with four-legged tickets', 'There's more thieving on the stock exchange than on the waterfront'.

Australian legends are always in temper democratic and

4

anti-authoritarian, about losers who might later win. That they pervade the attitudes of the whole society was understood by an American visitor who said: 'Australia is the only country in the world who could have a ten-dollar bill with a forger who was sentenced to death on one side, and a revolutionary poet who died a pauper on the other!'

Our yarns are usually ironic in tone, sometimes self-deprecatory (we are able to send ourselves up, as illustrated by 'Australians are the most wonderful people in all the world'). Sex appears infrequently and so do four-letter words which is contrary to the fetish of the modern stand-up comedians who seem to be influenced more by American than Australian traditions in humour.

The Australian yarn-spinner's world is a male domain, as I found when searching my archives. This is historically conditioned: in the pioneering days, men went away shearing or droving while the women minded the kids and the farm. In the shearing sheds and country pubs, the Australian yarn was thus born amongst the men; the women had no-one to yarn to and little to laugh about. Until the recent decades Australian women rarely told yarns. My sister Mary was the pioneer of women comedians in this country, and is much admired by the burgeoning group of brilliant women comedians now holding their own with their male counterparts. Women are minor characters in most of our myths (though this may change soon enough). Feminists might be consoled by my observations in 'The Great Australian Lover' which reveal that the insensitivity of Australian men and their treatment of women, and that their propensity to prefer the company of their mates, was much worse twenty years ago.

When Joseph Furphy asserted that his book *Such is Life* (Ned Kelly's last words, by the way) was in spirit 'democratic; bias, offensively Australian', he might have been describing the traditional Australian yarn. The very titles of some of the myths reveal their democratic nature: 'Never judge people by the clothes they wear', 'The Aussie battler is better known than the Pope', and 'The hunger for knowledge is a powerful thing' in every battler's soul so that he might do a course in Pelmanism in the middle of the desert.

The so-called tall-poppy syndrome is, at least in the view of Truthful Jones, a virtue, not a fault, in the Australian character as he brilliantly illustrates in 'They are the trouble'. The 'They' is authority, and Truthful vows to 'find out who they are . . . They'll get theirs and the world will be a better place with them not in it'. Cutting tall poppies down to size is an essential sceptics' way of keeping the bastards honest; suspecting them of all kinds of bastardry makes them take pause.

This scepticism also resists the Lucky Country trick: Truthful feels you need to be lucky to survive in the place, and reveals that the unluckiest man in the world was an Australian.

I once ran a yarn competition in my column in *People* magazine. Entries reflected the attitudes revealed in this book to the extent that variants of yarns I had told and published were sent in by readers apparently unaware of their origins; though, in some cases, it might have been a case of nothing new under the Southern Cross, because the yarn-spinner gathers as well as spreads yarns, and tales based on fact can emerge in different places without the story-tellers being aware of each other. Thus do myths spread and multiply!

Dogs and crocodiles were liberally sprinkled amongst the entries, so I've included Truthful's classic on these subjects.

The reader may have noticed that I speak of Truthful Jones as if he existed. When I first referred to him (circa 1966) in the ABC television program *Would you Believe?* listeners wrote letters to him, and *People* readers now do the same. If Truthful didn't exist, I would have had to invent him.

Without planning to, I have created four alter egos: Billy Borker, F. J. Borky, Ross Franklyn (about whom a film has been made and learned papers written in the universities)— and Truthful Jones.

In Truthful, I inadvertently created the perhaps archetypal Aussie battler, ironic, suspicious of authority, contemptuous of pomp and privilege. He sees something immortal in the ordinary bloke and 'the more they try to keep him down, the better he lives . . .'

Truthful's nationalism is not as aggressive as that of Joseph Furphy (there's something uncanny about the juxtaposition of those words: Truthful is used in the perverse way of Australian humour in which things are defined by their opposites and Furphy means a lie or rumour): he is sceptical about the Americas Cup malarky (perhaps as a reaction to the jingoism of 'They' in recent decades) and about all attempts They make to remythologise by equating themselves with the battler.

Especially, he is caustic about the destructive mythologising of the wheeler-dealer, take-over bid scammers as if they were the modern equivalent of Ned Kelly ('Ned died poor as well as game from bullets fired on behalf of Them').

The advertising jingle which says 'For all of you who've made it, this one's made for you', and all the other bullshit about winning, have become his targets. He reflects the bemusement and scepticism of the ordinary Australian: to him the new rich are less worthy foes than the old rich, if only because the new rich 'think manual labour is a Spanish bullfighter' and neither toil nor spin nor create any jobs or real wealth. So Alan Bond became Awful Alan against the tide of the phoney acclaim he generated by 'winning' the Americas Cup, which was really only 'the new rich racing the old rich, sponsored by the multinational rich, to bore the arse off the poor'.

Thus Truthful Jones brings the legend-based ideals into the present, from the bush to the cities, to combat Their attempts to remythologise the past and create new legends more in keeping with the outlook and aims of the rich and authoritative. He is also a wake-up to Their propensity to rewrite history, to lie about the past to influence present-day thinking.

He knows that Banjo Paterson stood for different things than Henry Lawson, who wrote from the point of view of the battlers of the legendary Nineties. He compares 'Waltzing Matilda' with 'Freedom on the Wallaby' unfavourably, and accused Banjo not only to have falsely claimed authorship of our 'unofficial national anthem' but also to have toned it down because he was, unlike Lawson, essentially one of Them.

His claim that the Jolly Swagman in 'Waltzing Matilda' was

7

a Bavarian anarchist named Samuel Hoffmeister will shock many; his assertion that Hoffmeister died by gunfire after an armed battle between shearers and police during which Hoffmeister had burned down the Dagworth woolshed will probably be met with disbelief. Yet readers may stop to think why three troopers were sent to arrest a swagman for stealing one sheep in a country where sheep-stealing was a way of life, and find more credible Truthful's claim that Hoffmeister was, in fact, to be charged with arson, sedition and conspiracy to set up an Anarchist Republic in Western Queensland.

Of course, a yarn-spinner is essentially an entertaining story-teller. His irony is perverse: he may not be interested in champion tennis-players, he may be contemptuous of yacht-racing, yet he boasts about the world's greatest grog-gargler who, needless to say, came from Darwin. Australians find alcoholic excess highly amusing; and turn one of its consequences, vomiting, into an art: hence the champion chunderer from Coopers Creek wins the Archibald Prize.

The yarn-spinner is much given to absolutes and hyperbole, as in the world's worst worrier and the legend of Crocodile Hogan. He relishes a good story and delights in the nuances of absurd detail and eccentric characters.

He is a myth-maker and creator of legend by accident; he says with Jean Cocteau: '*Je suis une monsonge qui toujours dit la vérité*'. With Truthful Jones it is a case of admitting: 'I'm a bigger liar than Tom Pepper—but my stories are all true'.

That Aboriginal myths are part of Australian folklore.

THE FIRST AUSTRALIAN BLACK AND WHITE YARN

Story-telling or yarn-spinning has been a popular pastime in this country for 200 years—that's if you only count white Australia. But if the rich oral history of the Aborigines is taken into account, you could say for 30,000 years.

Even in the first years of white settlement, Aboriginal yarns about the white invaders were a rich part of our folklore.

One of the first Australian yarns is about an Aboriginal named Musquito (spelt with a U instead of an O for reasons best known to the whites who eventually sentenced him to death). Musquito belonged to a Sydney tribe but was transported to Tasmania. At Port Arthur he was forced by the authorities to assist them to capture white bushrangers. Musquito's success in these endeavours earned him the hatred of bushrangers and convicts alike. So he managed to escape and join a tribe of Tasmanian Aborigines.

At first, Musquito imitated his white betters: he became a bushranger himself—and proved difficult to capture. Soon he became, with a Tasmanian Aboriginal warrior named Black Jack, leader of the last-ditch stand of some of the surviving Tasmanian tribes. Such was Musquito's skill in guerrilla warfare that the police called him the Black Napoleon.

Eventually, Musquito was captured by two white settlers. He was blamed for nearly every major crime that was committed during his period of freedom. Black Jack was captured soon afterwards.

They were tried on the same day in December 1824. They had no defence counsel and neither was fluent in English. Musquito was found guilty and sentenced to be hanged. For some obscure reason, Black Jack was acquitted, but was rearrested a month later and charged with the murder of a store-keeper named Patrick McCarthy.

Musquito and Black Jack were publicly hanged in Hobart Town on 24 February 1825.

By coincidence, six white bushrangers were hanged in the same bloody session. An historian of the time bemoaned that this was 'looked upon by many, as a most extraordinary precedent', presumably meaning that black fellas should not be seen to be equal to white fellas even on the gallows.

Musquito's reaction to the sentence was as startling as it was funny! He said to his jailer, a Mr Bisdee: 'Hanging's no good for black fella.'

Amazed, Bisdee said: 'Why not as good for black fella as for white fella, if he commits murder?'

Musquito replied: 'All right for white fella, him bin used to it.'

An historian guessed that Musquito meant that 'although executions were useful amongst the white people . . . who understood the reason of men being thus punished as examples for others, his execution was useless as an example to the Aborigines.'

I don't know what Musquito meant, except that his remark revealed that gap between the two cultures—as did his comment to the minister of religion on the scaffold. The minister suggested that Musquito should pray.

Musquito replied: 'You pray, boss, me too bloody frightened to pray.'

If that story is the first black Australian yarn, then here's the first white Australian yarn to survive in our folklore. It has become known as 'the great Australian joke'. There are many versions. Here's the one told by an old mate of mine, dead these many years, Billy Borker:

'Two old swagmen had been, for some time, silently carrying their swags along a road that led always to the horizon. As they were going nowhere in particular, they were in no hurry.

'They were men of very few words, named Bill and Jim. They began their aimless tramp one morning and Jim said: "It's gonna rain."

'Towards evening, Bill replied, "It ain't gonna rain!"

'A few mornings later, up a creek bed to the side of them, they passed a big black object which had clearly been dead for several days.

'About midday, Jim grunted: "Did yer see that dead ox?"

'As the shadows of the evening closed around their camp, Bill spat solemnly into the fire and replied: "It weren't an ox, it were a horse!"

'With those few words, he unrolled his swag and went to sleep. When Bill awoke next morning, Jim was gone. All Bill found was a grimy note stuck in a cleft stick by the embers of the fire.

'It said: "There's too many arguments in this bloody camp".'

2

That Australians would complain in heaven.

THE WORLD'S WORST WHINGER

There I was, drinking with Truthful Jones in the Billinudgel Hotel up the NSW North Coast.

Truthful appeared to have run out of yarns but I bought him a beer nevertheless and asked: 'Would these yarns you tell be peculiarly Australian, or would there be variants of them in other countries?'

Truthful Jones sipped his beer and replied: 'My yarns are all true . . . well, put it this way: every yarn is true to the yarn-spinner who's telling it.'

'I once heard a couple of your yarns in London,' I told Truthful.

'They must 'ave spread there by word of mouth,' Truthful replied.

'What would be the best Australian story you ever heard?' I persisted.

'Well,' Truthful replied reflectively, 'I reckon the most fair dinkum Australian story ever told is the one about the great Australian whinger . . .'

'I've heard of the whinging Pom—but never the whinging Australian . . .'

'The Australians will play the Pom on a break when it comes to whinging. The world's worst whinger was an Australian. I first met him—the world's worst whinger—in a shearing shed in Queensland during the Depression. I asked him an innocent question: "How would you be?" '

'Well, he dropped the sheep he was shearing, spat, fixed me with a pair of bitter eyes and says: "How would I be? How would you expect me to be? Get a load of me, will yer? Dags on every inch of me hide; drinkin' me own sweat; swallowing dirt with every breath I take; shearing sheep that should 'ave been dogs' meat years ago; working for the lousiest boss in Australia; frightened to leave because the old woman's lookin' for me in Brisbane with a maintenance order. How would I be? I haven't tasted beer for weeks and the last glass I had was knocked over by some clumsy coot before I finished it!" '

'He must have been a whinger, all right,' I said.

'The world's worst, like I told you. Next time I met him he

was in an army camp in Melbourne. He'd joined the AIF. "How would you be?" I asked him.

' "How would I be? Get a load of this outfit. Look at me flamin' hat. Size nine and a half and I take six and a half. Get an eyeful of these strides—you could hide a blasted brewery horse in the seat of them and still 'ave room for me. And get on to these boots, will yer? There's enough leather in 'em to make a full set of harness. And some idiot brasshat told me this was a man's outfit. How would I be? How would you expect me to be?" '

'Is this story true?' I asked.

'Well, most of my stories are true, but this one, you might say, is truer than true! I met him next in Tobruk. He was sitting on a box, tin hat over one eye, cigarette butt dangling from his bottom lip, rifle leaning on one knee, cleaning his fingernails with the bayonet. I should have known better, but I asked: "How would you be?"

'The whinger stared with malevolent eyes. "How would I be? How would you expect me to be? Shot at by every Fritz in Africa; eating sand with every meal; flies in me eyes; frightened to go to sleep expecting to die in this God-forsaken place. And you ask me *HOW WOULD I BE?*" '

'Did you ever meet him again?'

'No, he was killed at Tobruk, as a matter of fact.'

'Well, one thing, he wouldn't do any more whinging, poor devil.'

'You know,' said Truthful, 'I dreamt about him the other night. I dreamt I died and went to heaven. It was as clear as on a television screen. I saw him there in my dream and I asked: "How would you be, mate?"

'He eyed me with an angelic expression and he says: "How would I be? Get an eyeful of this nightgown, will yer? A man trips over it fifty times a day and takes ten minutes to lift it to scratch his knee.

' "And take a gander at me right wing, feathers falling out of it—a man must be moulting. Cast yer eye over this halo; only me big ears keep the rotten thing on me skull. And just take a Captain Cook at this harp—five strings missing and

14

there's band practice in five minutes! *HOW WOULD I BE?*
*HOW WOULD YOU EXPECT A MAN TO BLOODY WELL
BE???*" '

'A good story,' I admitted. 'Yes, a beauty.'

'The most fair dinkum Australian story every told,' Truthful Jones replied, downing the last of his beer.

3

That many Australians have had a leg bitten off by a crocodile.

THE LEGEND OF CROCODILE HOGAN

'I've been reading an article about the people taken by crocodiles in Australia, including that American tourist,' I said to Truthful Jones in the Harold Park Hotel.

'Yeh,' Truthful replied. 'Your Australian crocodile is the cleverest in the world . . .'

'Nothing clever about killing people; they're savage monsters . . .'

'Savage, yes, monsters, maybe; but clever, for sure,' Truthful replied, tilting his hat back and licking his lips. 'Which reminds me: did I ever tell you about Crocodile Hogan?'

'You mean Paul Hogan.'

'No!'

'Crocodile Dundee, then?'

'No, Crocodile Hogan. No relation to Paul Hogan or Crocodile Dundee; although I did hear that the character in that film was based on Crocodile Hogan.'

'You don't tell.'

'Positive fact. Crocodile Hogan was the greatest croc-hunter the world ever saw, would play Dundee on a break.'

I sensed a yarn, or even a myth. 'Have another beer and tell me about him.'

'I'll force one down, just to be sociable. The old Crocodile Hogan was like yourself: he hated crocodiles; but after hunting them for twenty years, he had to admit they were clever . . .'

'But crocodile-hunting is against the law . . .'

'Ah, the old Croc Hogan didn't believe in the law; didn't believe in the sack, either. That's why he gave up workin' for bosses, and took up hunting crocodiles: bosses had a habit of givin' him the sack, even though they knew he didn't believe in it . . .'

'Like Mitchell in Henry Lawson's story . . .'

'That's where he got the idea: told the boss he didn't believe in the sack, then told the coppers he didn't believe in the law against killin' crocodiles. Made a fortune—but two things worried him: that sheila who came from New York went for Dundee instead of him—and the crocs eventually got too clever for him . . . It was this way: Crocodile Hogan killed more crocs than Dundee and all the other Northern Territory liars in history—until the crocodiles started to wake up to his methods . . .'

'How could a crocodile understand the methods of a hunter?'

'By observation, that's how. He hunted mainly at night with a bright spotlight; the crocs used to be blinded by the light and just lie there until he shot one. But then they dived to the bottom as soon as he turned the light on. But the old Crocodile Hogan was on the cunning side, himself, so he hunted by day. Used to shoot a crocodile right between the eyes. Then he began to miss; couldn't believe it; often he'd put his second shot in the same hole as the first; now he couldn't make a kill with six shots. Months went by without Hogan killing one croc, and eventually there was a shortage of crocodile-skin shoes in the fashionable city shops . . .'

'This story better have a good ending; have another drink and get on with it . . .'

'Don't mind if I do. Anyway, the old Crocodile Hogan got

an idea: study the language of the NT crocodiles and find out what they were up to . . .'

'Here's your beer . . . first I ever heard of crocodiles talking . . .'

'You learn something every day. Hogan had often listened to them talking; lying in his swag wondering what they were saying. Told everyone in the Darwin pubs that crocs could talk. One day an Aborigine from one of the north-western tribes said they spoke a dialect of his tribal language. Hogan was usually a slow learner, but he picked up this lingo in a few weeks and headed upstream to where he had been shooting and missing all those months . . . So he made camp beside a croc-infested hole—and listened! Soon, two cunning-looking crocodiles surfaced downstream and one said: "Yeh, it's Hogan all right: the idiot's back. We'll play that old joke on the mug: swim side by side, a few inches apart with only one eye each showing above water." Well, Hogan couldn't believe his ears . . .'

'Not the only one,' I interrupted sarcastically 'All right, I believe you, but thousands wouldn't,' I added, knowing how upset Truthful could get if you didn't believe his stories. 'What did Hogan do, when he overheard how the crocs had been conning him with the two-eye trick?'

'Nothin' he could do: his rifle wasn't loaded, and it was near sundown. After dark, he got his powerful searchlight ready and when two crocs surfaced pretending to be only one, he aimed his rifle a few inches outside one of the eyes, instead of between 'em, and got one of the crocs. The crocodiles didn't think for one minute that Hogan could have learned their language . . .'

'I give up!'

'Ask yourself a question,' Truthful advised. 'How many white Australians can speak an Aboriginal language?' Then he answered his own question. 'About one in every half million, and that's a fact. And another thing, how many of 'em can speak any other language except English? Not bloody many, when you consider that we have people coming here who speak nearly every language on earth. Why don't we teach more foreign languages in the schools and try to learn the language of a Vietnamese or a Greek? Because we're racists at heart and have inherited from the Poms the idea: let 'em learn English or be forever dumb . . .'

'All right, get off your soap box . . .'

'Well, Hogan got a truck-load of skins, working day and night shift, on account the crocodiles didn't stop to think he had learned their language. Off he choofs to Darwin and sends his catch south. And there, in the Vic Hotel, who should he meet but Big Wheel his cunning self. So Crocodile Hogan taught Biggs the language and took him in as a partner for one trip. They were so successful that crocodiles really did become an endangered species. Big Wheel was a smart-Alec type, which led him to make a fatal mistake: he spoke to Hogan in the Aboriginal dialect within hearing distance of two old crocs. And the crocs spread the word: "don't use the two-eye trick any more, the white bastards are a wake-up to it." Anyway, they'd made a fortune and Big Wheel retired a rich man. Hogan had learned to respect the cleverness of the crocs, but that didn't stop him from hunting them. It's thirsty work . . .'

'Have another drink and get on with your awful yarn!'

'It's not a yarn, it's myth, or a legend. Anyway, Hogan used to listen to the crocs talkin'. One night he heard an old croc say: "Why does he kill so many of us?" Another croc replied: "Maybe because we kill a lot of people lately, too many Americans" and another said: "Maybe we should stop eating people and go back to dingos, cattle, and other four-legged tucker" and yet another: "And only snatch handbags from them Americans." '

'You must have seen the film about Dundee; but that was a camera, not a handbag, if I'm not mistaken.'

'Nothin' to do with Dundee: the crocs had heard Hogan and Biggs talkin' about crocodile-skin handbags and how well they sold. Anyway, Crocodile Hogan got really worried one night when he heard some crocs making a detailed plan to kill him. "Hogan must die!" the head crocodile said.'

'Here's your beer. If you must yak on; what did Hogan do?'

'That night he slept up a high tree; woke up when he heard an old crocodile yelling: "We know you're up there, Hogan;

come down and be eaten like a man." Then he heard a young croc comment: "I'd rather eat a Yankee tourist, any time: white Australians are too tough and we never eat black Australians, on principle." ' Truthful tilted his hat back and looked at me quizzically. 'You callin' me a liar?'

'Never said a word . . .'

'Well, did you ever hear of an NT crocodile killing an Aborigine? A'course you didn't . . . Anyway, Hogan heard the old croc say: "I'll get you a nice juicy Japanese tourist tomorrow when the boat arrives." Hogan was defiant. "I've got my tucker bag up here, so I don't have to come down for a week." The crocodiles waited while Hogan slept; a young crocodile volunteered to climb the tree. It slithered out of the water, up the tree-trunk—and grabbed Crocodile Hogan by the right leg. Two other crocs helped get Hogan into the water. Hogan was worried. "Tell you what," he said. "Let me go and I'll never kill another crocodile as long as I live." But the crocs didn't trust Hogan so, after a young buck says white Australian meat was too tough, they decide to bury Hogan in the mud to allow the meat to mature, that's to say, go rotten . . .'

'So they ate Hogan and every crocodile lived happily ever after . . .'

'Matter of fact, Crocodile Hogan grabbed hold of a long reed, put one end in his mouth and the other just above the surface of the water. When the crocs came back to eat him, he'd gone: snuck away during the night. Last I heard of him, he'd given up croc-hunting and started an SP book in Brisbane; hid his betting slips in an aluminium leg: that crocodile had bitten off his right leg when dragging him down from the tree.'

'It's a bit fantastic, but I'll use it.'

4

That you can't judge people by the clothes they wear.

NEVER JUDGE PEOPLE BY THE CLOTHES THEY WEAR

Truthful Jones was not very impressed when I told him about the book, *Great Australian Legends*, I'd been commissioned to write—until I offered him half the proceeds.

We met in the Carringbush Hotel to throw some ideas around. Truthful bought the first beers.

'What?' I asked, 'you win the Lotto or something?'

'We're partners now,' he replied. 'See that couple at the other end of the bar?'

I looked and saw a man with hair shaved at the sides and spiked on top, wearing punk clothes; a woman with multi-coloured hair and way-out clothes to match.

'Well,' I scratched my head, 'could be university drop-outs or members of a rock band . . .'

Truthful grinned. 'Or dole bludgers. Then again, he could be a computer programmer and she a hairdresser from Toorak.' He tilted his hat back and emptied his glass. 'Never judge people by the clothes they wear.'

I ordered more drinks. 'Is that an Australian myth? That we never judge people by the clothes they wear?'

'Judge for yourself,' Truthful replied. 'I'm gonna tell you a

true story that happened on Randwick racetrack, years ago. I went to the races to keep up my payments to the Destitute Bookmakers Fund. Before the last race, I'd put half me hard-earned in their bags, so decided to have a pie and carefully study the form.

'The meat pie is the staple diet for your Australian punter,' Truthful continued. 'He holds the pie to the leeward side with gravy running down one sleeve and tomato sauce down the other. So I ate me pie and sat down on the lawn near the fence of the Members' Enclosure—and study me bundle of form guides. The weights and distances confused me, so I decided to study the people in the Members instead, especially the ladies in their finery. They looked great, most of 'em. The men weren't so crash hot. Some of 'em wore those striped trousers and looked like Sir John Kerr on the piss at the Melbourne Cup.

'Anyway, I'm sitting there wondering how the hell I'm

going to get out on the last race when across the lawn walks an apparition. He was an old codger, the shabbiest man I'd ever seen in all me born days. His clothes wouldn't have brought ten cents at a garage sale: a threadbare overcoat; shoes with the uppers broken away from the soles—you could see his dirty bare toes; trousers with holes in the knees. He had a week's growth on, dirty face, hands and fingernails. He'd slept in the Domain under hundreds of copies of the *Sydney Morning Herald*, by the look of him . . .'

I hastened to buy another drink. 'Where the hell would he get the money to go to Royal Randwick?'

Truthful replied, after tilting his hat back: 'Well, the way I worked it out, the ticket sellers had gone off the gates and he'd wondered in just to have a sleep in the sun. I thinks to meself, poor old devil, and lookin' again into the Members, I cogitated on the inequality of the human race. Then the old man shuffled across the lawn with people lookin' down their noses at him and sits down. Silhouetted there against the white fence he held his feet up for all the toffs to see and waggled his dirty toes. He had a terrible look on his face like a man who had seen a lot of trouble in his time and had big worries on his mind.

'Well, I decided to go over and give him a few dollars to buy a feed. I'm headin' towards him when he started to go through his pockets, the worry lines on his face were those of a man haunted by want and fear. He put his hand in his inside coat pocket, still lookin' very worried. Slowly he pulled his hand out . . .'

I said to Truthful: 'Pulled out some scraps of food he'd rummaged out of garbage bins, I suppose.'

'No, he pulled out a roll of ten-dollar bills that would have choked a cow. But he still looked worried as he flipped through them, then put them back.

'Before I could say anything, he put a dirty claw in his other inside pocket and pulled out a roll of twenty-dollar bills that Winterset couldn't have jumped over. He searched through them, more worried than before, then pulled out a roll of hundred notes.

'He looked more worried all the time. The worry lines on his face were like spaghetti, so I could hardly see his despairing eyes. He went through his pockets again, searching and pulling out notes, but couldn't find what he was looking for . . .

'At last, almost in tears, he gropes for the fob pocket of his dirty old trousers, slides his thumb and forefingers in, and the wrinkles fell away from his face as if a facelifter had worked over his skull. And his face lit up with a smile of joy and contentment.'

'What did he find in the pocket?'

'A dirty old bumper, a cigarette butt no more than an inch long. And he said to me: "Have you got a match, mate?" I handed him a box of matches and he burned his nose lighting the cigarette butt, it was so short.'

'Where did he get the money?' I asked.

'How would I know. Won it punting, maybe. And don't ask me why he didn't buy himself a decent packet of cigarettes, because I don't know about that either.

'But ever since that day, after observing the old codger and the toffs in the Members' Enclosure, I've always said that you should never judge people by the clothes they wear!'

'It's a great Australian myth, Truthful,' I said. 'Never judge people by the clothes they wear. We're in business: I've got a few written already. We'll meet here tomorrow and work out some more . . .'

'Can I have my share of the advance on the book now—in cash?'

'No worries,' I replied. 'I backed the winner of the Golden Slipper.'

5

That money doesn't make much difference.

HOW MONEY CHANGED THE LIFE OF
SHEKELS MITCHELL

'I'm broke again: don't know where the money goes,' I said to Truthful Jones.

'Money doesn't make much difference. If you've got your health you've got everything,' Truthful replied. 'The only time I worry about money is when I haven't got any. And right now, if roast turkey were a cent an ounce, I couldn't afford a feather of a tomtit's tail.'

'It's no fun being broke,' I said.

'Being broke's not the worst of it. No man's so poor he can't get into debt. Being in debt is a way of life in this country. Do you know that every Australian owes $5,000 of the national debt and a thousand dollars to the hire purchase companies? Makes you think, don't it?'

'Yeh,' I replied. 'The rich are getting richer . . .'

'You've got to have money to make money, mate, that's the trouble. You know what the old Bible said: "To the haves shall be given and the have-nots shall be touched for their last cent." '

'I don't seem to recall reading *that* in the Bible.'

'Well, words to that effect, and those who work hardest earn the least,' Truthful insisted.

'I've read in the paper about the likes of Alan Bond who started with nothing becoming billionaires,' I argued.

'Don't believe everything you read in the paper; it's like I said, money doesn't make much difference.'

'I've never noticed you throwing it around.'

'What! I won the lottery once and spent the lot in six months. That's how it is with the Australian battler. If he gets hold of big money, he thinks it'll last forever, so he gets rid of it quick. He sticks to his mates, doesn't become a snob or anything like that, but pretty soon he's broke again.'

'Surely you've heard of a man who made money and hung on to it?'

'Yeh, I have, come to think of it. But it didn't make much difference to him. A fella by the name of Shekels Mitchell.'

'Have a drink and tell me about him. You always have a specific character in your stories.'

'That's because they're true, mate. Had a head on him like a burglar's torch,' Truthful began his yarn. 'A long thin neck and a round head. Every real character has a definite name and a head on him like something. I'll tell this story my way, see. But if you tell it to someone else, you can use a different name and say his head was like something else: maybe a robber's dog or a warped sandshoe.'

'But I thought you said the stories are true.'

'Every Australian yarn is true—for the yarn-spinner who tells it. Well, this fella Shekels Mitchell was always trying to make money. Believed all the stories about office boys becoming managing directors. He tried everything: selling gum leaves, hotdogs, home-made pickles, insurance policies, vacuum cleaners, encyclopaedias, and second-hand cars. He tried SP betting, interstate truck-driving, and chicken-sexing. But he couldn't get in front.'

'You said he eventually made money. Here's your beer.'

'It was a funny thing. He could never keep creases in his trousers.'

'And what's that got to do with it?'

'Got a lot to do with it. His missus used to nag him about it.

He tried everything, even putting his trousers under the mattress at night. Then he hit on an idea. A special trouser hanger that would keep the creases in your trousers. He invented this here trouser-hanger and began to manufacture them in a shed in his backyard. He put 'em on the market and they sold like hot cakes—that was before they invented these here stove-pipe trousers without creases.

'Anyway, pretty soon he had a factory and ten women working for him. That's the secret, mate, get other people working for you.

'Anyway, he gets an accountant to work out how much money he is making and one day he comes home and says to his missus: "Now, darling, I've got money. The accountant says I'm well in front. Is there anything you want?" "No, dear, all I want is you and the children." "I insist," he says, "you stuck to me during the Depression. Now I've got money, you can have anything you want." "Well," his missus says, "there *is* one thing. Everyone in the street has got a barbecue in their backyard." "Say no more," he tells her, "get one put in right away. The best in the street." So they get the barbecue put in.'

'Great idea, a barbecue; I'll put another beer on it.'

'Well, next June he comes home and tells his wife that the accountant has declared another dividend. "Just say the word, if there's anything you want," he says. "Well, darling, there *is* just one more thing." "Name it," he says. "Well," his missus tells him, "having the didee in the backyard isn't very convenient." "How right you are," he tells her, "get the plumbers in and build the best toilet that money can buy, right inside the house. Tiled walls, the lot. Spare no expense." '

'A man who spent his money wisely!'

'You can say that again. Trouble was, he got that way he could talk about nothing else except money. Used to get on his mates' nerves down at the club—always bashing their ear about how much money he was making, about having shares in the BHP, a barbecue in the backyard and a didee in the house. Kept it up, day in, day out. One of his mates got sick of this, see. So he says to Shekels Mitchell, "Listen, Shekels," he says, "you are always yakyaking about how much money you're making. What difference has all this money made?" '

'Well, the old Shekels thinks for a minute, looks a bit puzzled, then says: "Well, it hasn't made much difference at all, really. Before I had money I used to eat in the house and the didee was in the backyard. Now I eat in the backyard and the didee's in the house. Come to think of it, money doesn't make much difference." '

That some of the wealth of millionaires seeps down to the poor.

THE ONLY MILLIONAIRE WHOSE WEALTH SEEPED DOWN TO THE POOR

Truthful Jones was in the Harold Park Hotel watching television, when I came in.

'What,' I asked. 'You watching *Dallas*?'

'No, and it's got me stuffed how some battlers do watch it: millionaires screwing each other's wives. Matter of fact, I was watchin' a BHP advert . . .'

'That's even worse,' I replied, and bought a drink, and quoted. ' "The flagship of the BHP fleet that carries our exports . . . That's got to be good for all Australians." A variation of the old line of bullshit that what was good for General Motors was good for all Americans.'

'The ad said that BHP has the biggest goldmine in the world. That's all right for Australians, I suppose, at least for the blokes who work in the mines,' Truthful said.

He had touched a sore point with me. 'Don't tell me you believe the line that if the rich get richer, some of their loot will seep down to the poor—like Joh, Clint Howard and Bonnie Bob Hawke. They all agree on that and it's bullshit!'

Truthful tilted his hat back and bought a drink with a sly

grin. 'Well, I actually knew a bloke once who owned a gold-mine and a lot of his loot seeped down to the poor. Fella by the name of Joe Parsnip. Might be a myth.'

I was a wake-up to his tactics, since I'd offered him a split of my take from the *Great Australian Legends* book, but I let it pass. 'Joe Parsnip was a prospector who struck it rich, I suppose.'

'No, he was a shit-carter in Kalgoorlie; wouldn't have known a nugget of gold from a clinker of coal. But he had an Irish mate called Sandy Panter who could smell gold-bearing land a mile off . . . When they teamed up, Sandy sunk a shaft near a quartz reef north of Kalgoorlie. But Joe Parsnip was a know-all. "We should dig a hole over there," he said, pointing to rocky ground.

' "That's solid rock, yer spalpeen," Sandy replied and began to drive a shaft into the reef. Joe Parsnip blasted a shaft into the rock—and stumbled into a jeweller's shop.'

'What the hell's a jeweller's shop?'

'A hole in a rock in which minerals form over the centuries, looks beautiful, glistens like a jeweller's shop. That mineral can—once in a blue moon—be pure gold. When Sandy fainted on the spot, Joe Parsnip guessed he'd found a great nugget of pure gold. Worth nearly a hundred thousand quid it was, more than a million dollars in today's money . . .'

'Gold is where you find it,' I said. 'But it's scarcely a myth . . .'

'You ain't heard nothin' yet. Gold affects different people in different ways. It had a funny effect on old Joe Parsnip, the shit-carter. He was a tall lean man of doubtful age; been poor all his life; walked with his feet at a quarter past nine . . . Drank with the flies all his life because he stank and was a bore. Anyway, Joe Parsnip and his mate managed to lever the nugget onto the back of their old truck and drove into Kalgoorlie . . .

'They staggered into a pub and managed to dump the nugget on the counter,' Truthful went on. 'And Joe Parsnip yells out: "Fill 'em up! The drinks are on Joe Parsnip!"'

'Well, soon the whole town gathered and the pub stayed open all night with Joe buying the drinks. Next day, Joe Parsnip and his mate went down to the Government Assayer's Office, had the gold valued and eventually deposited their money in the bank. Some diggers get mean when they strike it rich but Joe Parsnip was the opposite. He gave up shit-carting and went on the greatest spending spree in history, after his mate, Sandy Panter, had gone back to Ireland. He bought a pianola and a big American truck . . .'

'I thought you said that Joe Parsnip's wealth seeped down to the poor.'

'Wait till I tell yer: for example, one day, Joe staggers out of the pub and hands the keys of his new truck to an old drunk sitting on the edge of the horse trough. "See that there truck? Well, it's yours, mate." The drunk replied: "I got no use for a truck; I can't even drive." Old Joe turned nasty. "When Joe Parsnip gives you a present, you take it, see." And he pushed the drunk into the trough. "If you can't drive it, sell it." Needless to say, hangers-on followed Joe wherever he went, while he kept boasting about his knowledge of gold prospecting, and saying he could find another nugget any time he wanted. A'course, he'd forgotten his mate had gone back to Ireland and he, on his own wouldn't have known gold from cow shit unless he tasted it.'

'Don't tell me he seeped all the money down to the poor . . .'

'Well,' Truthful insisted, 'he turned out to be a tit man from way back, so he proposed marriage to the barmaid with the biggest boobs and she accepted. "What would you like for a wedding present?" Joe asked. She replied: "What about buying me the pub?" And Joe did, on the spot.'

'Did they settle down in the pub together?'

'No, Joe Parsnip spent the next ten years trying to get it back orf her.'

'Go broke, did he?'

'Kept telling everyone he knew where there was another jeweller's shop, north of where the railway line cut out. So he went down to the railway station and told the station master he wanted to buy a train. "You can't buy a train," the man said. "But you can hire one . . ."'

'Joe Parsnip loaded the train with all sorts of mining equipment, beer, wine and champagne—and a hundred spongers.

Everyone was drunk and singing, including the train driver and conductor. At the end of the line, some followed Joe Parsnip into the bush.'

'Don't tell me Joe found another nugget . . .'

'The first one was beginner's luck,' Truthful evaded. 'Parsnip was soon stony-broke and without a friend in the world. But ten years later, in the same Kalgoorlie pub, a white-haired old man lugged a big nugget into the bar and said: "The drinks are on Joe Parsnip!" '

'And he spent the lot again?'

'I can't rightly say. I left Kalgoorlie a few weeks later. But I did notice, while I was buying my ticket, Old Joe Parsnip hiring another train, with a barmaid on each arm. Definitely the only time a millionaire's money seeped down to the poor.'

7

That the Aboriginals acted in self-defence when killing white men's cattle.

WHEN BURRUNJUCK MET THE TRIBE WITH THE SPLIT FEET

(As told to Frank Hardy by the late Lupgnagiarri, story-teller for the Gurindji tribe.)

Many years ago before I was born my grandfather, Burrunjuck, and my grandmother went out to get food.

They was no white man in this country in those days.

They went to hunt for emu or scrub turkey. They looked for tracks and they found these new fresh track and they caught up with him; and it was a cow and calf and them was drinkin' water by Wattie Creek.

My grandfather and grandmother wasn't realised what they was, that cow and calf.

So they was tryin' to get a word out of him. They asked him a few questions but the cow and calf only answered 'Moo!'

So my grandfather thinks to himsel': 'What I got here! A tribe with four legs and split feet?'

So them cow and calf can't speak a word of Gurindji language and my grandfather and grandmother went back to the camp and they told the elders what they bin seen.

Next eebning the whole tribe went out to Wattie Creek and they find a big mob of this tribe with split feet.

So my grandfather, Burrunjuck, says to a big bull 'G'day,' and all the bull said was: 'Moo!'

And Burrunjuck says: 'This not been your country, what country you come from?'

And the bull said: 'Moo!'

So Burrunjuck said: 'This bin Gurundji country. You can't come here drinkin' our water . . .'

And the bull said: 'Moo!'

So Burrunjuck and the elders had a good look at him. They wasn't gonna kill him or anything. Jes get a good look at what he was. Talk to him—but all he could say was 'Moo!'

Then all of a sudden a big bull he gave one of the elders of the tribe a kick up the arse and he went whoo, tipped him over so, of course, my grandfather, Burrunjuck, had to spear him.

Then they bin talkin' about this mob, not another tribe at all, but some kind of good tucker so they cut him up for beef and they ate him and it was good tucker. Them cattles had been bought here by Paddy Gale and Tommy Gale, they was the first white cattle men come to Wave Hill area.

Later on, one eebning, Paddy and Tommy Gale came over to the Gurindji camp and they had with them one Afghan camel driver. And my grandfather, Burrunjuck, bin watchin' 'em and they all got bald heads, Paddy Gale had no 'air, Tommy Gale 'ad no hair and the Afghan 'ad no hair.

So it was a very funny story: first there was a tribe with four legs and split feet, then another tribe with 'em with bald heads.

And Paddy Gale and Tommy Gale they went crook at that Gurindji mob. And my grandfather, Burrunjuck, told 'em, 'We was only tryin' to get a word out of 'em, find out what country they come from. We didn't want to kill 'em or anything but one big bull bin kickin' old man, knocked him on the ground, so I had to kill him with spear. Then we bin thinkin' maybe this mob not people, not some other tribe, but some bush tucker so we bin cut him up for beef.'

And Tommy Gale said: 'Yeh, but you bin killin' twenty or thirty of them cattle.'

Well, Burrunjuck knew that the Gurindji tribe, they eat

anything that walked around out there so they couldn't make out what Tommy Gale and Paddy Gale was tellin' 'em. Anyway, Paddy Gale and Tommy Gale set up camp and built a little homestead and they got all this cattle, hundreds of cattle.

One eebning, Paddy Gale and Tommy Gale came across to the Gurindji camp and they bin dressed up like blackfella. They got white paint and they got feathers stuck on they skin and they dance about. Reckon they proper Aborigines and they bin tell Burrunjuck and the elders of the Gurindji tribe, 'You can have plenty tucker, you can eat them cattles if you help me bin count 'em, put 'em in that yard there with the fence. Have as much tucker as you want, men and womens and childrens.'

So some of the Gurindji men they learn 'em to ride those horses that Paddy and Tommy Gale had with them and they bin soon roundin' up them cattle better than Tommy Gale or Paddy Gale. Put 'em in the paddock and Paddy and Tommy Gale bin show 'em how to put brand on 'em, so they did put brand on 'em.

And that's how the Gurindji tribe started to work for white cattlemen.

Later on that Bestey mob bin take 'em over that cattle station from Paddy Gale and Tommy Gale and the Gurindji kept workin' for them: and them been workin' the cattle and brandin' the cattle and the women, they bin work at the homestead in the kitchens and cleaning up and cooking.

But my grandfather Burrunjuck said: 'We never meant to kill them cattle and eat 'em. We thought they was another tribe with split feet and we tried to get a word out of 'em, tried to explain they should go back to their own country, but they couldn't speak a word of the Gurindji language. Neither could that Bestey mob. Not the Gurindji fault that they attacked them cattle. It was what you white men call 'em self-defence.'

Anyway, one eebning, later on, the Gurindji decide they not work for Bestey's any more and they go back to Wattie Creek and, when they short of scrub turkey or any other bush tucker, they bin cuttin' up cattle for beef.

So some white men came from the south with rifles and the

Gurindji run away up to Seal Gorge but the white men chase 'em and the Gurindji have to put up a bit of a fight.

And they did put up a bit of a fight. The only weapons they had was spear and nulla-nulla, and they had to fight a mob of soldiers.

My grandfather, Burrunjuck, had to try his best. He got five white men before they got him: dragged 'em down from the 'orse and kill 'em with his spear.

Then he came out of the gorge with him hand up. Thought they'd put him in gaol or something but they shot him through the heart—killed him.

No good blamin' the Aborigines for the trouble over cattle with the white men in them early days.

We live we own way at Wattie Creek; and work we own cattle.

And theys nothin' that Bestey's mob can do about it.

8

That Australian men are great lovers.

THE GREAT AUSTRALIAN LOVER

There I was drinking with Truthful Jones in the Carringbush Hotel, when the sex problem came up.

'There's more said and written about sex than football in this town,' Truthful said.

'Sex is important,' I defended.

'Of course it's important, but the old Henry Lawson himself summed it up: he reckoned you shouldn't make a problem of love—you should just make it.

'In every bloody magazine you pick up, you'll find articles on the sex problem—and sex gadgets: orgasms, real and contrived, vibrators, G-spots, foreplay and afterplay, decorated condoms, singles bars and doubles sex . . .'

I interrupted Truthful: 'They reckon the trouble is that Australian men are afraid to express emotion and love . . .'

Truthful emptied his glass. 'They wouldn't know. The trouble is that Australian men—and women—are encouraged to study sex as if it had nothing to do with love or emotion, like they were gymnasts . . .'

Truthful looked at me slyly. 'It's a thirsty subject, this . . .'

I took the hint and ordered two beers. 'Some Australian

women complain about Australian men and their attitude to sex, y'know, Truthful.'

Truthful sipped his beer. 'I never had any complaints. And you reckon you can outscrew as well as outwrite men half your age—so you couldn't have had any complaints, either.

'The Sex Problem in Australia is not the men's fault and it's not the women's fault. It's history's fault.

'Yer see, in the old days men went away droving cattle, fencing, shearing, and the women were left alone on some small farm, running it and lookin' after the kids. The women and the men were separated. And that's when I reckon men got their ballsed-up ideas about women.

'A woman was either a good little woman at home waiting for you while you travelled around earning a living, or she was a whore in some shanty.

38

'It takes a long time to overcome an attitude like that. Some Australian men still want their women to be angels, but they forget to try to be saints.

'Women were at a great disadvantage in this country, and the sexual revolution didn't help them much: male chauvinism took on a new guise. But that's all in the past now. And I'm one of the pioneers who changed it . . .'

Truthful Jones glanced at me. I sensed he was in full flight on a subject he didn't often discuss, the sex problem. Truthful continued—when he saw me order another beer.

'Y'see, more than twenty years ago I decided to send up Australian men and their attitude to love and sex. I made up a lotta yarns and told them, and some of them even got on television and into the newspapers. One was called "The Great Australian Lover". A satire on Australian men.

'The Great Australian Lover's name was Curly, who had a bald head. His mate's name was Burly, who would have weighed about thirty kilograms wringing wet in an army overcoat with house bricks in the pockets.

'The subject of marriage came up between them in the pub one Saturday morning . . .

' "You get married today, don't yer, Curly?" Burly asked, looking up from his form guides. "Next Saturday," replied Curly. After some debate, Burly reckoned, "It's terday, Curl, at noon. We've just got time to catch the first at the TAB before you go to the barrier for the Mug's Stakes."

'The TAB queue was long, and so was the wait at the church for the bride, who was dressed in white, and her parents, who had travelled a thousand kilometres specially for the occasion.

'During the ceremony, Curly's mother-in-law-to-be got technical and commented that the groom and best man should have worn suits instead of shorts, T-shirts and thongs.'

'The bride's mother was a bit narrow-minded, eh?' I urged Truthful Jones on.

'The bride's father was just as bad: he asked where the reception would be held. "Ah, we'll go over to the pub lounge and have beer and pies," Curly told him.

'The bride's parents didn't stay long. Anyway, Curly and

Burly filled the boot of their bomb with stubbies of beer for a party to celebrate the solemn occasion. All their mates came; some brought wives or sheilas. The bride came, too. The men stood at one end of the room telling dirty yarns; at the other, the women talked about what drongos their menfolk were.

'There were quite a few fights, a drinking contest and a fair bit of chundering. The bride, who was also inclined to be narrow-minded, started to cry for some reason, and locked herself in the bedroom.

'When Curly woke up with roadmap eyes and a mouth like the bottom of a cocky's cage, he was under the kitchen table. Burly was on the sofa. "Musta been quite a party," Curly said, surveying the empty bottles and full bodies on the floor.

' "What was it in aid of?" "You got married," Burly replied. "Where's the bride, then?" asked Curly. "In the bedroom, a bit upset."

'Curly knocked on the bedroom door and paled when a woman's voice answered: "Go away. I never want to see you again." "Ah, come on, darl, we'll 'ave to go on the honeymoon, won't we?" "Where are we going?" the bride asked Curly. "Hayman Island," Curly replied, and this brought the bride out. "I got three tickets." "What do we want three for?" "Well, Burly's coming with us. He's me mate." "If he comes, I'm not going." "Suit yerself," replied Curl.'

'Now I've heard everything,' I told Truthful. 'What happened after that?'

'Curly took Burly to Hayman Island. After a week, Curly sent a telegram to his wife: "Having a marvellous time but bad trot punting please wire one hundred dollars."

'The marriage didn't last, for some reason. But Curly and Burly are still the best of mates. A'course, that story happened a long time ago. But I helped Australian men wake up to their bloody selves. Now, Australian men, and women, are learning to treat their opposites as mates as well as lovers. You wouldn't get a better-looking, more intelligent or sexy person than the average Australian woman. And you and me—and Curly—can guarantee that Australian men are great lovers.'

That Australian women always have the last word.

THE LEGEND OF LAST WORD LAURA

Truthful Jones had just finished a very funny yarn about a big pumpkin and the two *men* who grew it when I said to him: 'Truthful, old mate, why is it that nearly all of your yarns and most of mine are about men?'

Truthful rubbed his chin, tilted his hat back, and emptied his glass. 'Well, you can't be talkin' about Rodney Rude and this latest crop of male comedians around the town. Nearly all their yarns are about women—as sex objects. Rodney is a genuinely funny man but he's got it into his head that unless he says "fuck" every five seconds no-one's gonna laugh at him . . .'

I interjected. 'Yeah, I'm talkin' about yarn-spinners, not one-line comedians. You'd better have a drink while I bore the arse off you with my theory about this question: that an Australian can't tell yarns, unless they're about dogs, crocodiles or horses. It was this way, I reckon, the first Australian yarns were amongst the convicts—and the men and women were separated (that's if you don't count the marvellous Aboriginal myths that have been here for 30,000 years before us white mugs turned up) then, as exploration of the back country spread, men travelled away from home and the women stayed at home minding the farms, like Lawson's drover's wife . . .'

Truthful interjected, 'Yeah, I've heard it all before, and the women stayed home and told fairy tales to their children which were not as bad as the fairy tales the men told them when they came home again. But there was another thing, even in the cities, until very recent years: men-only bars. Well, I heard a few women comedians the other night in Melbourne and they were bloody brilliant. I admit women yarn-spinners are still rare but, as they learn most of our other bad habits now that they're gettin' a bit more equal, they're bound to pick up yarn-spinning as well. But I've always told a lot of yarns about women, and without makin' them sex objects— well, not all the time . . .'

I pushed Truthful's full glass along the counter and decided to challenge him suddenly. 'Tell me an original yarn of yours about a woman, where she's not a sex object, go on!'

Truthful sipped his beer, gave his old napper the best scratchin' that it ever had, tilted his hat further back; then his eyes lit up and his mouth turned sideways in a gleeful smile. 'I'll tell you, mate, the best bloody yarn about a woman that's ever been told in the world—and she's not a sex object, either. Her name was Laura, Laura Langdon. They eventually called her Last Word Laura—and she earned every bit of that beautiful nickname.'

'I'm all ears.'

'Well,' Truthful said. 'This old farmer was drivin' along the Pacific Highway near St Ives in Sydney when his horse took it in its head to drop dead. And there he was with a dead horse and a cart full of milk and pumpkins in the middle of the road. Needless to say, hundreds of cars drove past; the flashest ones splashin' him with the most water . . .'

I interrupted. 'And what the hell has an old farmer with a dead horse got to do with a woman who's not a sex object?'

'Just because we live in a patriarchal society and you yourself are an idiot, and just because my yarn begins with an old farmer with a dead horse, there's no reason for you to jump to conclusions. It's a thirsty argument.' Truthful glanced at me with a sly grin.

I bought a drink and said: 'Get on with the story, Truthful!'

Truthful said, 'Never disturb a person when they're sleepin', makin' love, or workin'—never but never interrupt a yarn-spinner in the middle of a yarn, just because you think he's not gettin' to the point quick enough. Anyway, who should come along in a red sports car but an elegant lady who actually stops with a sympathetic ear. The farmer looks at her with her dangling earrings, beautiful evening dress, dazzling eyes and white teeth, and he says: "Me 'orse is dead and I can't shift it or the cart orf the road." To his amazement, the good lady took a tow rope from the boot of her car, secured the horse and dragged it off the road. She then took hold of one of the shafts of the cart and said to the farmer: "Come on, my dear chap, give me a hand." The farmer was utterly bewitched as he helped the lady to pull his cart into the wet grass on the side of the road—although, admittedly, he was a bit upset when the hem of her dress became wet and muddy. Then the farmer was utterly amazed when the lady proffered her delicate hand and said: "My name is Laura, what's yours?" The farmer took her proffered hand and said: "Jack . . ." '

'So her name was Laura—but how did she become known as "Last Word Laura"?'

Truthful scowled. 'That's what the bloody yarn's all about, mate. Laura says to Jack: "Jack, I'll give you $500 for your horse!" And Jack said: "But it's thirteen years old—and it's dead as well." Laura replied: "It doesn't matter, I'll give you $500 for it—if you'll help me get it to my house." '

'The plot thickens!' I exclaimed.

Truthful ignored the interruption. 'Well, the farmer thought he had enough on his hands but the good lady Laura proceeded to tie the other end of the tow rope to the back bumper bar of her car so as they could drag the horse along behind. Then she opened the door of the long red sports car and Jack got in. By the time they got to the double-storeyed mansion in St Ives they were on first-name terms for sure. Laura pulled up the car and said: "Just wait a moment, Jack,

I'll go around to the garage." She came back with an axe and a crowbar and passed the axe to Jack. Then she got stuck into one of the gate posts with the crowbar.

'By now Jack was a bit on the nervous side, to say the least, but he bashed down the other gate post with the axe (it was one of those flash gates with expensive lamps on the top of each picturesque gate post; be worth $5,000 if it was worth a cent). When Laura untied the tow rope and began to drag the horse through the gate Jack thought enough's enough.

'He asked Laura: "Can I have me $5,000 now?" Laura assured him he would get his $5,000 after he helped her get the horse into the house. They did about $10,000 worth of damage getting the horse through the front door and Jack got a dose of the jitters: "You can 'ave me 'orse for nothin'. It's thirteen years old anyway." Laura said: "A deal is a deal, Jack. When we get the horse up that spiral staircase you can have your money."

'That spiral staircase was worth $20,000—that is until Laura and Jack wrecked it with the crowbar and the axe. They dragged the horse up on to the landing, into the bathroom and after wrecking the door and the screen, into the bath.'

'This story better have a good ending,' I said.

'Downstairs, Jack asks again for his 5,000 bucks and Laura said: "First, we are going to have a whisky. I'm married to the greatest bloody know-all that ever God put breath in. He is a rich broker but he has got the brain of a baboon, yet he has to have the last word about everything. I've been married to him for fifteen years, brought up two kids, went back to university and became a Master of Arts—but he still doesn't listen to a word I say and has the last word on every subject. In five minutes he'll come out and go to the toilet in the bathroom.

'Jack sipped his whisky and they waited. Sure enough, the baboon broker went into the bathroom. Then he came to the top of the stairs and called out: "Laura! There's a horse in the bath!"

'And Laura says with gusto and glee: "Tell me something I don't bloody know!"'

I laughed appreciatively. 'And that's how she got the name of Last Word Laura.'

'Yes,' Truthful said. 'A story with a woman central character—and not about sex.'

'Did it really happen?' I asked.

'No,' Truthful replied. 'Only a myth: the Legend of Last Word Laura—to prove that Australian women always have the last say.'

10

That Australia is the lucky country but Australians are the unluckiest people in the world.

THE UNLUCKIEST MAN IN THE WORLD

'How did you go at the races Saturday, Truthful?' I asked.

'Lost again—for the eighth meeting in a row.'

'I've never backed a winner in my life. I'd be about the unluckiest man . . .'

'No, you wouldn't. A bloke I knew years ago was the unluckiest man in the world. He was so unlucky that when it was raining Paris night-clubs he got hit on the head with a Woolloomooloo plonk shop. He was an Australian, needless to say. You know why they call Australia the Lucky Country?' Truthful answered his own question. 'Because you need a lot of luck to survive in it.'

'You're not often wrong but you're right this time,' I commented slyly.

'Am I ever! Most Australians are unlucky but they never admit it or, rather, they never myth it; they think talking about bad luck causes more. But this fella kept grizzling about it all the time and there's nothing worse than an unlucky man who can't keep his troubles to himself.'

'Have a drink and tell me about him,' I said.

'I'll force one down just to be sociable. This fella was so

unlucky that one time he bought a bargain suit with two pairs of trousers and the first time he wore it he dropped his cigarette and burnt a hole in the coat. Moaned about it for weeks. The blokes at the pub got sick of his moaning. They'd say to him: "What about taking a share in a lottery ticket?" "I'm too unlucky," he'd say. Wouldn't even buy a ticket in a two-bob raffle. Every time the pub raffle was about to be drawn, they'd ask him to buy a ticket. "Not on your life," he'd say. "I'm so unlucky that, if it was raining mansions, I'd get hit on the head with a Charters Towers dunny." '

'Here's your beer. I suppose some people are unlucky.'

'You got to make your own luck, mate, that's what I always say. If a man gets convinced he's unlucky he'll bring bad luck on himself. Like this character I'm telling you about. He was always beat before he started. Anyway, there was a bloke used

47

to drink with him who was one of those do-gooding types whose main hobby is poking their noses into other people's troubles.'

'Kind-hearted people.'

'Maybe they are kind-hearted. More likely they're just sticky noses who get a kick out of other people's troubles. They used to call this do-gooder I'm telling you about "Good Turn Smith". If you can't do a man a good turn, never do him a bad one, he used to say. And he decides to do a good turn for this unlucky fella. "We'll run a big raffle," he says one Friday, "and we'll rig it so this unlucky character wins it." He reckoned that might restore the bloke's confidence and stop him from moaning about his bad luck. So the lads take up a collection of $100 and decide to raffle it for a dollar a ticket. They spread the word that the raffle is to be a sort of testimonial for the unluckiest man in the world. So they buy a raffle book specially made with every ticket number seven.'

'What good would that do?'

'Ask yourself a question. Their plan was to sell him a ticket which would be number seven, naturally; then draw the raffle: when the ticket came out of the hat it was sure to be number seven.'

'The plot thickens.'

'Trouble was, he refused to buy a ticket. "Not me," he says. "I went into the kidnapping business once and started off by kidnapping an orphan. I'm the unluckiest man in the world." Well, you can imagine how old Good Turn felt. Specially organised a raffle so's the unlucky fella could win it and he wouldn't buy a ticket.'

'You've got to be in it to win it, as the saying goes.'

'That's what Good Turn Smith said to the unluckiest man in the world. But he wouldn't be in it to win it.'

'Ah, now I get it. He's so unlucky that when they rigged a raffle for him, he refused to buy a ticket.'

'There you go again, trying to make me get ahead of my story. My father always said never get ahead of your story. As it so happens, that's not the ending of the yarn at all. Good Turn Smith argues with him, see. He says: "Tell you what, if you'll buy a ticket, you can draw the lottery yourself." "Be your age," says the unluckiest man in the world. "If I draw it I'll have no chance." "Come on," says Good-Turn. "We've sold a hundred tickets at a dollar. I'll put 'em in my old hat and you draw the raffle. Might change your luck." "It'll take more than that to change my luck. I have to wear braces as well as a belt or my trousers would fall down. The only time I backed a winner at the races in my life I lost the ticket and the TAB refused to pay me," says the unluckiest man in the world. "It's no use arguing with me. I'm so unlucky if I paid for a raffle ticket I'd be struck dead on the spot." "Well," says Good Turn, "in that case I'll pay for your ticket. There it is, number seven, your lucky number." "Lucky number? I'm so unlucky that I'm the only man in the world who hasn't got a lucky number. I went to the trots once in the afternoon and backed a horse each way in the last race. It ran third in the first race at the dogs that night—but there were only seven runners."'

'Not a man with a lot of self-confidence, I should say. Probably had an inferiority complex.'

'I get thirsty every time I tell this yarn. Old Good Turn Smith got upset too and he says: "Look, mate, I'm trying to do the right thing. I've paid for the ticket. The least you can do is take it as a present." And the unluckiest man in the world says: "I don't want to hurt your feelings but I'm so unlucky that one time when I went to a petting party with six of me mates and seven go-go girls, I got paired off with my old aunt."'

'Unlucky all right.'

'Wait till I tell yer. Old Good Turn does his block. "Listen," he says. "I've paid for the ticket. If you don't take it I'll ram it down your throat." The unluckiest man in the world never turned a hair. "I'm so unlucky," he says, "that if that number seven was the winning ticket you'd ram it down me throat and I wouldn't be able to collect the hundred dollars."

'Somebody says: "Ah, give him away, Good Turn! He's the unluckiest man in the world and no mistake." But old Good Turn was a stubborn man when it came to doing good turns. He gets a cunning look on his face and he says: "Tell you what. You take the ticket and draw the raffle yourself. That way you can't win, being the unluckiest man in the world like you say."

'That should have convinced him.'

'Yeh, Good Turn had found the formula. "All right," says the unluckiest man in the world. "Can't do any harm that way. No hope of my winning if I draw the raffle."

'So old Good Turn puts all the raffle butts into his hat, shakes it just to show everything was over and above board, and holds it high in front of the unluckiest man in the world. Old Good Turn was happy as a skylark. He says aside to his mates: "It's a matter of psychology. He'll win the hundred dollars and change his luck."

'The unluckiest man in the world reaches up his claw into the hat, stirs the ticket butts all marked seven and draws one out.'

'Won the raffle and changed his luck. Not a bad yarn. We'll have another drink on the strength of it.'

'Well, you can imagine the shock they all got when the unluckiest man in the world looks at the ticket and says: "What did I tell yer? I'm too unlucky to win a raffle even with a ticket someone else paid for."'

'How could he lose? All the tickets were marked number seven.'

'The unluckiest man in the world holds up the ticket he drew out and says: "What did I tell yer? I'm a quarter of an inch off a hundred dollars. I've got number seven and the winning ticket is six and three-quarters."'

'You're pulling my leg again.'

'No, true as I stand here. The unluckiest man in the world had pulled out the size-tag on the hat. And if you don't believe me you can ask Good Turn Smith. He ought to know.'

11

That the Aussie battler is better known than the Pope.

THE GREAT AUSTRALIAN LARRIKIN

'What would be the greatest Australian legend, Truthful?' I asked in the Carringbush Hotel.

'You mean the greatest Australian yarn?' Truthful tilted his hat back with his right thumb and continued. 'Only one in it: the great Australian larrikin.'

'Why would a yarn about a larrikin be a great Australian legend?'

'Because Australian humour is based on the battler: you can't win but you've got to battle. A'course, Alan Bond and his mob in television and advertising are trying to change the Australian attitude towards battling; they want to say that all Australians are winners, are going to make it. Whereas, the tradition is that you're not gonna necessarily make it, but you've got to battle, you've got to try, you've got to play the game even if you don't expect to win. The battler I'm tellin' yer about was called Dooley Franks.'

'Have another drink and tell me about him,' I said as I bought another round.

'Don't mind if I do. This fella was a real knockabout. Lived here in Parramatta. Ran a double, did a bit of urging at the races, sold smuggled transistors. One night he went to Tommo's two-up school and won 500 quid backing the tail. So he decided to join the Tattersall's Club. Up he choofs to the uniformed flunkey at the club door, wearing a polo-neck jumper, suede shoes, and one of them small-brimmed hats with a yellow feather in it. "Here, fill in this form," the flunkey says dubiously. "The committee will consider your application and let you know in due course." When the committee meets, the secretary says: "This Dooley Franks is an urger. We can't have him in the club." The committee members could not have agreed more: most of them *used* to be urgers, see. "Dooley Franks hasn't got two pennies to clink together. Just tell him the joining fee—a hundred pounds—and that'll be the end of it."

'So they write Dooley a letter and he bounces back and slams a bundle of tenners on the counter in front of the flunkey. Well, the committee got really worried. The secretary says: "Tell him he has to have three sponsors, famous people, not Australians. The furthest he's ever been from Parramatta is to the Kembla Grange racecourse." They think they've got old Dooley Franks beat, see. So the flunkey tells him: "Three famous people, not Australians." "Why didn't you say so in the first place?" Dooley says. "Would have saved time and trouble. Eisenhower [he was President at that time], Khrushchev and the Pope. Just tell 'em Dooley Franks from Parramatta wants a reference."'

'He was joking, of course?' I asked.

'Wait till I tell yer. Don't spoil one of the best Australian stories ever told. Well, the committee got a shock, needless to say. Now, the secretary was a hard case, so he says: "Listen, this here Dooley Franks couldn't know Eisenhower, Khrushchev or the Pope. Tell you what we'll do. We'll offer to take him over to Washington, Moscow and Rome, in person. Then we'll hear no more about it." They write to Dooley and he says: "All right with me. Air letters would be cheaper, but if you insist." The secretary says: "We're stuck with it now. We'll put in a hundred quid each and I'll go with him. It'll be the joke of the century."

'Away they go by air to Washington, up the steps to the

52

White House. They wait around in corridors for about three days and eventually they get an appointment with one of Eisenhower's side-kicks. "I'm from Tattersall's Club, Sydney," the secretary says. The Yank is puzzled. "Sydney?" he asks, "where's that?" "Australia," the secretary tells him. "Ah, yeah," the Yank replies. "That's where we sell all our old films to the television stations." "We want to see President Eisenhower," the secretary says. "You can't just come here and see the President. You have to have an appointment."

'Well, Dooley Franks is getting a bit impatient, see, so he says: "Listen, just tell Ike Dooley Franks wants to see him. The bloke who pinched six tins of petrol for him when his car ran out on the road to Paris. Dooley Franks from Parramatta." Well, the Yank goes away and comes back. "Mister Franks," he says, "why didn't you say so in the first place? President Eisenhower will see you right away." "Can I come too?" the secretary says. "No, the President wants to have a private chat with Mister Franks."'

'Surely he didn't actually know Eisenhower?'

'Well, he came back six hours later, high as a kite. "Sorry to keep you waiting," he tells the secretary. "Me and Ike got talking about old times over a few drinks and lost track of time." So they head off for Moscow.'

'Ah, don't tell me . . .'

'Up to the Kremlin gates with an interpreter they go. Freezing cold night, thirty-eight below. The secretary puts over a spiel about the Tattersall's Club and Dooley tells the bloke on the gate: "Just tell Nikita that Dooley Franks from Parramatta wants to see him. Was treasurer of the Sheepskins for Russia appeal during the war, sailed on the North Sea convoys and sold Russian magazines on the Sydney waterfront."

'Well, to cut a long story short, the same thing happens: Khrushchev wants to see comrade Franks, and the secretary of the Tattersall's Club is left freezing in Red Square. Dooley comes out eventually, and next day they head for Rome. And the secretary is thinking: "What will I tell the committee when I get back? They'll never believe me. If he gets in to see the Pope, I'm going with him."'

'And did he?' I asked.

'Well, they see a cardinal, but he says you have to make an appointment for an audience with the Pope. So Dooley tells him: "Just say Dooley Franks from Parramatta; was an altar boy at St Patrick's Cathedral, got a brother a priest and a sister a nun." The cardinal comes back—if you don't believe you can ask old Dooley himself—he says the Pope will grant a private audience to Mister Franks.

'The secretary begs to be let in. "I must see them together," he says. "His Holiness wishes to see only Mister Franks. But if you want to see them together you can stand down in the square. His Holiness will appear on the balcony at one o'clock and I'll arrange for Mister Franks to stand with him."

'Well, the secretary is desperate: what's he going to tell the committee? He goes away and comes back at one o'clock. The square is packed with 50,000 people. The secretary is so far away he can't even see the balcony. The crowd cheers. There's a Yankee tourist standing nearby with a pair of field-glasses. The secretary begs him: "Lend me your field-glasses." The Yank says: "They're not field-glasses, they're binoculars. And you can't borrow them. I've come 10,000 miles to see the Vatican . . ." The secretary says: "Well, what can you see?" "Two men standing on the balcony," the Yank tells him. The secretary tugs his arm. "Can you recognise them? Who are they?" The Yank takes a good look through his binoculars: "Well, I can't place the guy in the funny hat but the other guy is definitely Dooley Franks from Parramatta."'

I emptied my glass and bought another drink. 'So the Aussie battler is better known than the Pope.'

Truthful replied: 'Call it a myth or a legend, if you like, I call it a yarn that is truer than truth itself.'

12

That there are more eccentrics in Australia than anywhere on earth.

THE POGO-STICK MEN

Australia has ceased to value its eccentrics; yet it has more of them than any country on earth. Many Australian eccentrics have become national legends in their own time: take Bea Miles and Rum Jungle Jack White—and the man who stencilled the word ETERNITY on Sydney footpaths for fifty years.

Perhaps the most eccentric of all the eccentric Australians were the pogo-stick men; they used to repair the telegraph lines between Alice Springs and Darwin years ago.

No-one knew their names, so they were called Burly and Curly. Burly was a tall skinny fella and Curly had a bald head (he was no relation to Curly, the Great Australian lover).

They were men without pasts. No-one knew where they came from, but guessed that they came to the Northern Territory because Territorians don't ask people about their pasts.

In the old days, the Territory was a favourite hiding place for many men and a few women who had taken what was known as a 'working-class divorce': go to the corner shop to buy a packet of cigarettes, and buzz off to the Territory and avoid legal expense and alimony. Of course, others were escaping from other kinds of pasts.

For the pogo-stick men, the job on the telegraph line was a perfect cover: Curly was a 'wife starver' and Burly a bank robber who got caught by a bank teller with a wooden leg, then absconded from bail.

People first became aware of them when they saw two men camped by the road beside a heap of empty beer bottles as high as a camel's hump.

Curly and Burly would shop in the nearest town, then get on the booze. Eventually they would leave with their old truck laden with groceries—and uncountable crates of Victoria Bitter. The tales of eccentric behaviour which began to spread through the pubs in the Territory didn't worry them. Like all eccentrics, they saw nothing abnormal in their lifestyle.

They never read a newspaper but stole from pubs or general stores magazines which they would read from cover to cover, at least once. They even read the advertisements.

And one day Curly said: 'Burly, old mate, there's an ad for a barber's chair in this magazine. Mail order! Do you think we oughta write in and buy it?'

Burly replied: 'What would we do with a barber's chair?'

'Well,' Curly replied with an impish grin, 'you know what a hell of a job it is to shave in the morning. We go for days without having a shave. If we had a barber's chair, you could shave me, then I could shave you—every mornin'. We'd look better!'

Burly replied: 'Why should we worry what we look like? Nobody ever sees us—except truck drivers and tourists.'

Curly replied, 'Well, there is the good name of the Post and Telegraph Commission to think of. If we were cleanshaven the image of the Commission would be improved.'

Anyway, they decided to fill in the coupon in the magazine, go to the nearest post office and send a money order to buy the barber's chair.

When the chair arrived, they shaved each other every day.

Curly was what is known in Australia as a practical joker. He had played every joke known to the jokers of the world on Burly (except short-sheeting his bed and that was only because they had no sheets); now he decided to lather Burly with sandsoap instead of shaving cream. Burly took umbrage and refused to be shaved any more.

Not wanting the barber's chair to go to waste, Curly thought of the first of several ideas to play jokes on passing tourists.

He announced: 'Burly, me old cobber, I'm going to shift the chair to the side of the road. I pinched a white sheet out of the Katherine pub and I'm gonna use it for a barber's sheet to put around your neck while I give you a shave and a haircut.'

'Come orf it, Curly, I've cut me own hair all me life and I'm not lettin' you shave me in that barber's chair after what you done. I'll have a shave when I want to have one—and I'll shave meself.'

But when Curly explained the purpose of the public shave and haircut and swore he would use only shaving soap, Burly laughed and agreed to the experiment. 'Better you play your awful jokes on tourists instead of me.'

Camped in a very isolated spot at the time, not a house or a human being for miles around, they stood with their spanking new barber's chair beside the bitumen road.

So one day, when traffic was a bit heavier than usual (that is to say, a vehicle went past every half hour or so), Curly settled Burly down in the chair with a sheet around his neck. Curly had a pair of scissors jutting out of the pocket of his white shirt. He took out his cut-throat razor, brush, and shaving soap and proceeded to lather Burly up.

Curly kept lathering away until he heard a car coming. Then he placed a piece of toilet paper on Burly's shoulder and proceeded to shave him, brushing the whiskers and soap off the razor on to the toilet paper, for all the world like a professional barber.

He shaved with great flourishes, until Burly became a bit scared that he might cut his throat.

And there was Curly in the middle of nowhere playing the part of a barber shaving a customer in a fair dinkum barber's chair, when over the hill came a car full of southern tourists. Curly shaved away, ignoring the car when it pulled up beside them.

One of the yobbos in the car said to Curly: 'This is a funny place to have a barber's shop . . . be bloody few customers around here . . .'

Curly replied: 'You mind your business and I'll mind mine. I'll set up me barber's shop wherever I like,' and he went on with his self-imposed task.

Well, the tourists had a good laugh and drove away.

Curly was cutting Burly's hair when a bus-load of tourists came along. The bus driver stopped and asked: 'Can I get a punk hair cut orf yer, mate?'

Curly replied, clicking his scissors, 'We kill punks up here, mate, and use their carcasses for poisoning dingos.'

The scene was repeated a few times until Burly ran out of hair. Curly tired of the joke anyway, and turned to playing jokes on publicans, instead of tourists. He rang up Darwin and sent a hearse to a publican who was harassing them for being too far behind with their payments. Burly expressed concern: 'We can't afford to offend publicans.'

So Curly said to Burly, 'There's an ad in this magazine for a pogo stick, mail order. What the bloody hell's a pogo stick?'

'Haven't got a clue,' Burly said. He was very fond of the term and it has since spread throughout Australia. How many times have you asked the time or the way to the post office and received that reply, a sign that people don't care any more? 'I haven't got a clue' seems to mean: 'I don't give a stuff about you and if I knew the answer to your question I wouldn't tell you.'

Anyway, even though Burly didn't have a clue about pogo sticks, Curly made a few judicious enquiries in the Tennant Creek Hotel, filled in the coupon and sent the money order south to Adelaide ordering one.

The pogo stick arrived, and Curly began to practise. It wasn't as easy as the advertisement had claimed but, after many falls and much derisive laughter from Burly, Curly mastered the gentle art of hopping around like a kangaroo. In fact, he became so fast that he was thinking of writing to *The Guinness Book of Records*.

Instead, he decided to play what must be one of the funniest and greatest practical jokes ever played in the history of human endeavour.

He said to his mate, 'Burly, I've got an idea for a joke on these bloody tourists, especially them Yanks that are always worried about runnin' into kangaroos. They are warned before they leave the Alice to watch out for kangaroos after sundown because if you run into a big ten-foot kangaroo you can wreck your car and kill yourself.'

'I haven't got a clue,' Burly said.

'The next time you say "I haven't got a bloody clue" I'm gonna flatten yer!' Curly retorted. 'But 'ere's me idea. You go down the road a bit, hide behind the bushes after the sun goes down and give me a yell when a car's comin', and I'll hop across the road on me pogo stick.'

And so it came to pass that Burly hid in the scrub and gave his mate the signal that a flash car was coming and Curly, with perfect timing in the falling light, hopped quickly across the road in front of the car on his pogo stick and disappeared into the bushes.

With a screech of brakes the car pulled up and Burly crawled through the scrub to join his mate in hiding. They lay in the bushes listening to the reaction of the occupants of the car, who turned out to be a Yankee tourist and his missus.

The first words Curly and Burly heard came from the wife. 'I tell you it was a man on a pogo stick.'

They heard the husband reply with a disdainful air, 'It was a kangaroo: they warned us that kangaroos move across the road towards nightfall. Anyway, what would someone on a pogo stick be doin' out here in the middle of the god-damn desert, you stupid woman!'

The wife insisted, 'I tell you, Egbert, it was a man on a pogo stick—not a kangaroo!'

The American couple got out and began to search the bushes, arguing whether they would find a kangaroo or a man with a pogo stick. They found neither because there wasn't a kangaroo within a bull's roar, and Curly and Burly lay doggo behind one of those big Northern Territory anthills.

Eventually, the American tourists drove away, still arguing bitterly whether they had seen a kangaroo or a man on a pogo stick.

Curly liked to tell variants of that story around the pubs. He even speculated on the effect of his simple act of hopping across the road could have had on the marriage of that couple.

Thus, Curly and Burly became legends in their own lifetime—and that was before the famous negotiations between Curly and his long-deserted wife.

She found him after making enquiries in every pub from Alice Springs to Darwin. The locals were very cautious about giving information to outsiders, but somehow she managed to establish that it was her husband and none other who worked with the tall skinny fella named Burly on the telegraph line. She sent a message to Curly with a truck driver and they arranged to meet on the side of the road to negotiate alimony.

Eventually Curly agreed to accept culpability and offered his wife, Nell by name, a settlement: one automatic lay-back barber's chair, one dozen crates of Victoria Bitter, one pogo stick, one ticket in the Queensland Lottery, twenty-seven old issues of *People* magazine with the crosswords unused, a post-dated cheque for 10 per centum of maintenance arrears—and a tin mine.

Curly and Nell, having reached agreement after much haggling, went to the bar to have 'one for old time's sake' then repaired to the bridal suite upstairs to have another 'one—of a different variety—for old time's sake'.

Nell headed south next day, never to see her husband again. 'Me and Curly are still in love,' she told her friends. 'It's just that we get on better if we don't meet too often: once every ten years is ideal for us.'

She reckoned it was the most generous, amiable and sexy divorce settlement ever reached—that is, until Curly's cheque bounced and the tin mine turned out to be full of water. It wasn't because Curly was mean; he just couldn't resist playing practical jokes.

Nell wasn't too pleased but, as she said, 'After all, I can't complain; I fell in love with him because of his sense of humour.'

Curly and Burly lived happily ever after. At last report they had ordered a billiards table by coupon from Adelaide.

I wonder why the media has lost interest in eccentrics. Could it be that the establishment feels threatened by them? Eccentrics are non-conformist and, in these days of census-taking and identity cards, their behaviour could lead to civil disobedience.

13

That the friend of today is the enemy of tomorrow.

THE LEGEND OF BAYONET BATES

'Do you think there'll be a nuclear war?' I asked Truthful Jones.

'More likely to be a non-nuclear war—there's about a dozen going on at the moment, like Iraq–Iran. And they're terrible enough. There's no such thing as good war or a bad peace, that's what I always reckon. I was in the 6th Divvy, mate, so I know what I'm talking about. They said we'd make the country fit for heroes to live in—and you have to be a bloody hero to live in it these days. I'll never fight in another war . . .'

I could not resist saying: 'You'd be too old, anyway.'

'That's lovely, that is; I'm as good as ever I was. Y'know, I know a bloke who actually fought in, not two, but *four* wars. Fought in the First World War, and the Second World War, then put his age back—and fought in the Korean and Vietnam wars.'

'Must have been a bloody patriotic bastard and no mistake.'

'Not patriotic at all. Just loved fighting and thought he might as well get paid for it. He said to me when he was leaving to go to Vietnam: "Who are we fighting this time,

Truthful?" The old Bayonet always got confused about who he was fighting, but he joined up regardless. And you must admit modern war is a bit confusing. We fought with the Russians in the first and second wars; now we're crook on 'em. The Japs were on our side in the first war and against us in the second—and now they're our biggest trading partner. We fought against the Germans in two wars and now we're building them up to fight on our side in the next.

'Old Bayonet Bates couldn't keep track. Funny part of the Old Bayonet; he's no respecter of nations or people; he'll kill 'em all without fear or favour. He always said: "A friend of today is an enemy of tomorrow." So he just gets stuck in and kills them all without fear or favour. They made a film of him in Vietnam. A film of him as the first Australian to make a kill there, for the BBC Television.'

'Did he get a medal?'

'The Old Bayonet got more medals than a Yankee general. On Anzac Day he has to have a crutch under his left arm . . .'

'War injury?'

'No, the crutch is to help him carry the medals on his left lapel. Did I ever tell you about them making the TV film of Bayonet Bates?'

'No, have a beer and tell me about it.'

'The Old Bayonet is going out on patrol and this here BBC bloke, Harold Hornblow, goes with him to make a film of the first kill. And he says to Bayonet: "Do you think you will kill one? I'd love to film it." And Bayonet says: "I'll kill one all right. I hate Japs," and Hornblow gets upset and he says: "We're not fighting the Japs this time." "Why doesn't someone tell me these things?" says Bayonet. "If I'd of known we weren't fighting Japs I would've went to Nicaragua. But, anyway, there's an enemy here that I'll find and kill. I hate the bastards.

'Hornblow was real pleased and he told his cameraman to be ready.'

'Here's your beer. Did Bayonet Bates kill a Vietcong?'

'Wait till I tell yer. "I hate 'em," he kept saying. "I hate 'em. I was the first Australian to register a kill in the Korean War and I'll be the first in the Vietnam War. I hate 'em." Well,

Hornblow has got the camera and sound equipment right on the Old Bayonet. And they're going through the jungle and Bayonet is saying: "I hate 'em. I can smell 'em a mile off. There's one around here somewhere."

'That's what he used to say during the Korean War: "We have to kill them up there before they come here." Trouble was, he couldn't tell the difference between a North and South Korean. So he killed 'em all. Both the North and South Korean governments gave him a medal before it was all over. And he's telling this to Hornblow as they're going through the jungle and he's saying: "It's hard to know which side you're fighting on. But I hate 'em. There's one around here and I'll kill him. Have you got a Bible with you, mate?" And Hornblow said: "Sorry, old chap; I left it back at head-quarters." And Bayonet said: "I s'pose it doesn't matter but they did say we should have a bayonet in one hand and a Bible in the other. I've got me bayonet but I haven't got a Bible."

'So they're going through the jungle and Bayonet says: "There's one." "Where?" cries Hornblow. Bayonet answers: "Over there in the jungle." Hornblow couldn't see anyone, but Old Bayonet could. He raises his rifle and takes careful aim. "It's one of 'em, all right. I hate 'em." And he shoots. "Got him," he says. And Hornblow rushes over with his cameraman and he comes back, furious, and says to Bayonet Bates, "Look at what you've done, you fool! I'll have you court-martialled for this. You've killed one of our gallant allies. All I can find over there is an American provost sergeant with a bullet between his eyes." And the Old Bayonet says: "I told yer I could smell 'em. I killed the first one in the Korean War, and now in this one. They'll give me a medal for this, won't they?"

'It's like I said: modern war is very confusing.'

'Yeh,' I said. 'But the most important thing is that the friend of today is the enemy of tomorrow.'

That Australians are the world's worst worriers.

THE WORLD'S WORST WORRIER

'Australians are the greatest race of worriers since the fall of the Aztecs.' Truthful Jones was sitting in the bar of the Billi-nudgel Hotel, where all the posh people and yahoos hang out up the North Coast.

'How do you make that out?' I asked, buying another round of drinks. 'One of Australia's main idioms is "No worries". And your average Australian laughs a lot.'

'He's laughin' and can't afford it,' replied Truthful. 'The Australian laughs to hide his worries. The sad clown, so to speak.'

I decided not to interrupt again; when Truthful is in full flight on a promising theme you don't interrupt him—except to buy a drink.

'Well,' Truthful Jones continued, 'there was this fella who couldn't stop worrying. He worked overtime at it. The lowest-paid clerk in the biggest office in Martin Place. Worried when he couldn't balance the stamp money; worried when it balanced, because he must have made a mistake. Worried he might get the sack; worried he might get into a rut if he stayed in the job too long. Worried because he had no children; then worried that he might have children and not be able to bring them up right. Worried that his wife might be unfaithful to him; and worried that she must be a dull woman when other men took no interest in her. Worried because he thought people were talking about him; and worried because people weren't interested in him.'

I bought another beer—and Truthful took a big gulp of his without missing a word. 'He had an anxiety complex so big that Phar Lap couldn't have jumped over it.'

'If he ever stopped worrying, he worried because he had nothing to worry about. It got so bad his wife started worrying because he was worried; and he started worrying about his wife being worried. Then he started worrying about the nuclear threat—and that really sent him around the bend. So he went to one of those shrinks. Then he started worrying

about how he'd pay the psychiatrist's bills. Then a funny thing happened: he won the bloody Lotto!'

I bought another drink and commented: 'And at last he stopped worrying.'

'Not him,' Truthful Jones proceeded. 'He started to worry what to do with the money. Lay awake at night thinking people would touch him for it. Well, one day one of his mates at work, a bit of a hard case, said: "What are you worrying about? You've got plenty of money; why don't you employ someone to do your worrying for you?" So he puts an advert in the paper. *Worrier required. Only experienced men need apply. Excellent salary.*

'And he got one reply. A little skinny fella with worry lines all over his face and haunted eyes. Had good references, too. Been bankrupt twice. Married twice and both his wives left him, which worried him a lot for some reason. A bigger worrier than his new employer, if that was possible.

'Of course, the world's worst worrier had to make sure he had the right man. He was going to pay big money. He asked him a lot of questions, but he couldn't fault him. At last he asked: "Do you bite your fingernails, like me?" And the applicant replied: "I'm such a worrier, I bite other people's fingernails."

'Well, that clinched it. He gave him the job and stopped worrying on the spot.

'Then he took his wife for a trip to the Barrier Reef. He never worried. Always bright and cheerful. Stopped biting his fingernails.

'Made his wife the happiest woman in Australia. If he got a worry he just referred it to the professional worrier. He became the most happy-go-lucky man in the world.

'One day his wife said to him: "I hate to worry you, dear, but the bank manager's just rung up and, because you're paying that man so much to do your worrying, all your money's gone and you're in debt." '

Truthful Jones studied his empty glass and gazed through the door at the banana-coloured sunset (as Patrick White would have said) and delivered the punch line: '"No use tellin' me that," the world's worst worrier replied. "That's his bloody worry." '

That Australians will not admit to being illiterate.

THERE'S NONE SO BLIND AS THEM THAT CANNOT READ

'What are you whistling?' I asked Truthful Jones in the Carringbush Hotel.

'Slim Dusty song: "When the Rain Tumbles Down in July". Wrote it himself.

'"The Pub with No Beer" made him famous.'

'His best song is the one about the Aborigine who died drinking at the poisoned waterhole just because he couldn't read. The pastoralist made him foreman but didn't ever teach him to read.'

'Illiteracy is a terrible thing,' I replied. 'Ten per cent of the white population of Australia can't read or write.'

'Yes, and they say there's none so blind as them that cannot read.'

'Here's your beer. Who said that?'

'Well, old Paddy Murphy from Cooktown never—and that's for sure. He couldn't read but always pretended he could. Used to pretend to read the paper. Sometimes he'd hold it upside down. A bloke looked over his shoulder one day and saw he'd got the paper upside down. There was a picture of a ship in full sail. "Anything in the paper?" he asks old Paddy. "Ah, nothing much," says old Paddy. "Another shipwreck, that's about all." '

'You're getting worse; a bigger liar than Tom Pepper!' I exclaimed. 'Whoever he may be. Have another beer.'

'The story's true, and I can really prove it this time. Old Paddy Murphy lived in Cooktown, in the far north of Queensland, in the old days. Back before my time—but I can still prove the story is true. Well, he couldn't read. People soon woke up to him but he still pretended he could read. Made a lot of money out of a goldmine, built himself a big house, but too mean or stupid to learn to read. It was the joke of the town—people asking him what was in the paper, and how to spell long words, but Paddy kept pretending. He had a mate who could read, who used to read his mail for him and not let on about Paddy being illiterate, but this fella went prospecting on top of a place called Mount Poverty, miles out of town. If Paddy ever got a letter he'd say to the man at the post office: "Could yer be after reading that letter for me? Oih've left me glasses at home." Well, as luck would have it, old Paddy never got any mail for a long time, but he used to sit on the verandah of his house in the main street pretending to read a book or a newspaper. Everyone was a wake-up to him but Paddy really thought he had them convinced he could read. He used to go down to the post office regular as clockwork, but no letters came. He began to worry, thinking some of his relatives might have died, or maybe the post-master was stealing letters addressed to him that had money in them.'

'How did he get on about signing his name?' I asked.

'Well, it was a funny thing. His mate had taught him years before to write "P. MURPHY" in block letters but that was all the writing he could do—and he couldn't read a word. Anyway, a few local wags decided to play a joke on Paddy, who wasn't very popular in the town on account of being so mean; and this pretending to be able to read was getting on people's nerves, as well. So they go up to his house one night. It was a stone building with a big hardwood front door. They wrote something on the door. Next day Paddy sees the writing, but can't make head nor tail of it. So he thinks: "I wonder what's written there? Maybe someone's left me some money. People

69

I knew down south know I can't read, though I've got all these local spalpeens convinced, bad cess to 'em. Maybe someone down south has sent a message and the locals have written it on the door . . ." He gets real upset.'

'What was written on the door?' I asked.

'There you go, trying to make me get ahead of my story again. I never spoil the ending just because some mug gets impatient. I can't tell you what was written there without spoiling the ending.'

'No offence meant.'

'And none taken. It's just that I have to tell the story properly. Anyway, old Paddy's real cunning, see, so he waits until someone comes past his house and decides he'll trick them into telling him what's written on the door. Along comes the first bloke and Paddy starts laughing: "Look what some fool has gone and been after writing on me front door." This bloke knows all about the sign so he says, "It's no laughing matter, Paddy," and away he goes. "No laughing matter!" Paddy thinks to himself. "Me poor old mother must be dead and me not writing to her ever in me loife and her believing I learned to read and write in Australia."

'So along comes another bloke and Paddy pretends to cry. This bloke is in the know, too, so he says: "It's no use crying over spilt milk, Paddy," and he goes on his way. "Spilt milk!" Paddy thinks. "What's he mean by that? P'raps I've lost a fortune on the shares I bought in Brisbane."

'Then along comes the woman from across the street. Paddy says to her: "There's some fools in the world, Mrs Rafferty: look what some spalpeen has gone and wrote right across me front door." Mrs Rafferty is no friend of Paddy's, so she says: "It was no fool who wrote that, Murphy, as God is my judge."

'While Paddy's trying to work out what she means, along comes another woman. "Look what's been wrote on me front door," says Paddy. "It's no laughing matter, is it? No use crying over spilt milk, eh; and it was no fool who wrote it, or my name's not Paddy Murphy." The woman tells him: "You should think very carefully about what's written there,

Paddy." By this time the whole town has agreed not to tell Paddy what was written there unless he asks straight out.

'He tried every trick he could think of: laughing, crying, joking; he even offered to buy two little kids some lollies if they told him, but it was no use. By nightfall, old Paddy was beside himself with curiosity and worry. He was convinced that his mother was dead, that he'd lost his money, that he'd inherited a fortune, that he'd been given a decoration by the Pope. Suddenly, he thought of his mate who was prospecting on top of Mount Poverty seven miles away. His mate'd tell him what was written and no questions asked. He couldn't wait until the morning, so he thinks of a bright idea. He takes the door off its hinges.'

'What good would that do?' I queried impatiently.

'He decides to take the door up the hill to his mate. As true as I stand here, and I can prove it. It was a heavy, hardwood door, like I told yer, but old Paddy, who was not a day under seventy, carried it seven mile uphill, like Moses carrying the tablets of stone up the hill to meet the Lord.'

'Moses carried the tablets of stone *down* the hill, Mount Sinai, *after* he'd met the Lord.'

'I stand corrected. Paddy carried it on his back, under his arm and balanced on top of his head; the trip nearly killed him. But he never carried it down like Moses, he was too tired after carrying it up. Took him all night. He arrived at daylight and staggered into his mate's camp. "For the love of God, mate, tell me what's written on this bloody door," he begs, and he pops the door against a tree and collapses on the ground.

'If you don't believe this story, mate, you can go to Mount Poverty any time you like and you'll find right on top of it a big hardwood door with no house around it; just the door standing there on its own. There was a photo of it in the paper the other day.'

'But what *was* written on it? That's what I want to know.'

'Well, the writing has faded with the weather after all these years, but they tell me if you squint close enough you can read it.'

'And what does it say?'

'Why don't you admit you can't read, you Irish bastard? And if you don't believe me you can go and read it for yourself. It's like I told yer, mate, there's none so blind as them that cannot read.'

16

That Australia has the highest beer consumption in the world.

THE WORLD'S GREATEST GROG-GARGLER

'Tell me the most awful Australian yarn,' I said to Truthful Jones in the Victoria Hotel, Darwin. 'I've got the mother and father of a hangover, so speak softly. Went to my son Alan's birthday party last night. Have a hair-of-the-dog with me.'

Truthful rubbed his chin. 'You've got road-map eyes, a mouth like the bottom of a cocky's cage—and a stomach like an active volcano! Right?'

'Spot on!'

'Well, then, in your state of health, I can't tell you the most awful Australian yarn ever told—I'll tell you the second most awful. The yarn is called "The World's Greatest Grog-gargler". He lived in Darwin. The official statistics show that they drink 254 litres a year in Darwin for every man, woman and child. The highest consumption in the world.

'One night in the Buffs Club, they were having a drinking competition to see who would wear the toaster's collar. The competitors were lined up to see who could down a pint the fastest, when this quiet, unassuming fella leaned on the bar and says: "Do you mind if I have a go?" 'The president said: "Be my guest."

'This bloke grabs a 1.3-litre jug and downs it before any of the others drink a pint. He never took the jug from his lips but they could hear a strange gargling noise.

'The boys from the Buffs knew they had the new Darwin champ on their hands and nicknamed him the Gargler.

'The reigning Darwin champ was a bloke at the Workers' Club, who drank eleven bottles in twelve hours.

'The only rule was a no-spew one—perhaps chunder is a better word.

'Well, a judge was appointed by the Licensed Victuallers Association to see fair play.

'The champ drank his first eleven in seven hours and seemed to be going easy when he chundered on the floor. He was disqualified under the no-chunder rule.

'The Buffs Club decided to give the Gargler a go at the twelve-bottle record.

'The Gargler—a very modest fella despite great achievements—said: "I'd have to try meself out first to make sure I can do it—before you start betting on me."

'From midnight, he drank a bottle an hour on the hour right through until midday without turning a hair.'

'Did he eat anything?' I asked.

'No, and he never showed any signs of chundering either.

'The boys asked him: "When will you start?"

' "No time like the present," he says. "I'll start now and go through till midnight."

'The word spread through Darwin like rain in the wet season, and thousands of dollars were laid out in side wagers.

'Through the afternoon and into the night the Gargler gargled on and progress reports were spread by couriers: "He's on his fifth bottle and going easy," and "He drinks a whole large bottle without taking it from his lips," and "He has a glass or two in between to quench his thirst." '

'Have another drink. You're making me feel thirsty,' I said.

'I'll force one down just to be sociable. Anyway, the Gargler drank the twelve bottles in ten hours.

'No-one in Darwin would try their skill against the Gargler after that, so a few of the lads took him down to Mt Isa.

'As soon as some of the Mt Isa mob started to boast about

drinking, the Gargler modestly suggested a test of skill and endurance under LVA rules—no food, no chunder.

'Well, they cleaned up good money for a while until the local champion challenged the Gargler to a contest, drinking 1.3-litre jugs from a standing start for a side wager of $500.'

'Here's your beer,' I said. 'The Gargler must have been a big powerful man to drink all that beer.'

'It was a funny thing that; he was a little skinny fella. But he had two things in his favour that made him the world's greatest grog gargler. He had a pot belly and no epiglottis.'

'What's an epiglottis?'

'It's the thing in your throat that makes drinking a slow process: he had no swaller, that's what it actually amounted to. Anyway, they stand with their hands behind their backs and a jug in front of each of them on the counter.

'The judge said: "Go."

'The Gargler finished his before the other bloke got halfway. He drank it in 7.2 seconds flat, according to the official timekeeper.

'Of course, they couldn't get a bet on in Mt Isa after that. So they head for Alice Springs, but word of the Gargler's exploits had spread ahead of them so they couldn't get any money on.

'Then the Gargler said: "Tell you what I'll do, gentlemen. Just for a friendly game, I'll drink on me own against a team of eight. First to finish an eighteen-gallon keg is the winner."

'No man in the world could beat an Alice team on his own. But the Gargler did it.

'Next they went to Tennant Creek and there the local champion says: "I'll drink him under the table, if we mix the drinks. We drink every drink on the shelf in order: beer, advocaat, cherry brandy, whisky, and so on."

'The Darwin mob had never seen the Gargler drink anything except beer. But they backed him and he won again.

'Then a very strange thing happened,' Truthful said, pushing his empty glass towards Jill.

'You don't mean to say! Don't you call what you've been telling me strange?' I exclaimed.

'The Gargler decided to give up competitive drinking. "It's

no use arguing with me," he told the mob from the Buffs. "I'm retiring undefeated champ of Australia. It's a matter of principle; we're taking people's money under false pretences." '

'But I thought you said the Gargler eventually became world champion. Have another and get this awful yarn over with.'

'The Gargler read in the paper that Yankee soldiers on leave from Vietnam were running what they claimed to be a world championship chug-a-lug in Hong Kong.

'A chug-a-lug is a drinking contest. The Yanks named it after a song recorded by Roger Miller: "The Chug-a-lug Song". Anyway, the Gargler gets upset.'

'Reckoned he should be world champion, I suppose.'

'Not only that: he was crook on Yanks for some reason.

'People said his wife had run away with a Yankee provo on R&R from Vietnam. His Darwin backers had him on a plane for Hong Kong within a week. There were fifty entries for the championship and the Gargler didn't try too hard during the early rounds so they could get plenty of money on in the grand final.

'He drank off the big fat Yankee provo sergeant and the side bets ran into thousands of dollars.

'It was the Gargler's finest hour. He just kept one drink ahead while his mates kept laying bets like a two-up school. They drank beer and rye whiskey.

'The Gargler gradually drew further ahead until the Yank chundered over one of the judges and was disqualified.'

'And so the Gargler became world champ. I don't believe a word of it,' I said.

'The Yanks believe it, mate. The Gargler and his Darwin mates fleeced them for months.

'The American command issued a routine order-of-the-day about the Gargler: "To all troops going on leave to Hong Kong. The steep fall in morale of combat troops in Vietnam is thought to be due to certain drinking contests being conducted.

' "Troops are advised not to enter into such contests with an Australian of dubious character who wears a drinking bib on which the words THE GARGLER are inscribed.

' "This man is believed to be an enemy agent endeavouring to undermine the health and morale of American troops." '

'If that order was ever issued — which I doubt — it would put an end to the Gargler's career, fleecing our gallant allies,' I said.

'It put an end to the war, as well. America pulled out of Vietnam because the Gargler had ruined the health of so many of their crack combat troops,' Truthful adds.

'That's the worst yarn I ever heard,' I told Truthful.

'The second worst,' he replied.

17

That vomiting is an art.

THE CHAMPION CHUNDERER FROM COOPER'S CREEK

'What are you laughing at, mate?' Truthful Jones asked.

'Can't help laughing every time I think of that story you told me yesterday about the Gargler, especially the bit about the US Army Routine Order telling the troops not to drink with him,' I told him.

'No more than a simple fact of history, mate. I know an even better yarn called "The Champion Chunderer from Cooper's Creek".'

'You'd better have another drink and tell me about it.'

'Well, this particular fellow actually started off as a grog-guzzler, just like the old Gargler himself did. That's how it is with people: they never quite get into the right profession. They tell me Ed Clark, the US Ambassador, wanted to be a rancher, then he found an oil-well by mistake and decided to go to night school to study to be a horse doctor and instead of that he ends up a diplomat. Then Sir Robert Menzies himself wanted to be a whisky-taster at the Melbourne Show, but ended up as some kind of wharfie over in Pommy Land.'

'Here's your beer. Then there was that violinist you told me about who wanted to be a League footballer. Where did he come from again?'

'A place called Chinkapook in Victoria. People are never satisfied and that is where human progress—if any—comes from.

'Anyway, this here chunderer from Cooper's Creek wanted to be a professional grog-guzzler. He got the idea from hearing about the exploits of the Darwin Gargler. So he heads into Alice Springs to try himself out against the champs of the Alice (he'd beaten all comers in Cooper's Creek, which was no mean feat, I can tell you). And he won a few hundred dollars in the Alice, beat all their best men; standing start on the jugs and the endurance test on the bottles. So he decides to head for Darwin to challenge the Gargler himself.

'But one of the Alice Springs guzzlers says: "Listen, mate, you're wasting your time going to Darwin. That bloody Gargler's got no swaller. You couldn't beat him with an axe. Anyway, they've got a no-chunder rule in Darwin. All their

THE MORNING AFTER

79

contests are under the auspices of the LVA and they're very strict on the no-chunder rule. You've chundered your heart up after every contest here; you wouldn't reign for a week in Darwin, mate, and that's for sure."

'But the Cooper's Creek champ wouldn't be told and off he choofs to Darwin to challenge the Gargler. But the Gargler had already left for Hong Kong in his laudable attempt to end the Vietnam war. Anyway, the Cooper's Creek lad gets into a contest on the fifty-two-ounce jugs here in this very bar.'

'Have another drink and get to the point.'

'The point is how he switched from grog-guzzling to this profession he was born for, chundering, and I'm coming to it right now. He beats one of the Vic champs, but the judge from the LVA follows him to the didee and hears him chundering. "You're disqualified for chundering," he yells out over the cubicle door. And who do you think walks in at that very moment?'

'Haven't the vaguest idea. Here's your beer.'

'None other than Crooked Bed McCracken himself.'

'Not the bloke who used to exhibit the Wild Man from Borneo?'

'The man himself over from North Queensland for the Darwin Show. He was looking for someone to exhibit as the Wild Man, but couldn't get any volunteers. And in he walks and he says to the judge: "Listen, mate, is your name Herb?" The LVA man says his name isn't Herb and Crooked Bed says: "Well, that bloke in there is calling for Herb." '

'I don't get it, how do you mean—"Calling for Herb"?'

'Well, you've heard a bloke having a good chunder, saying "Herb . . . Heeeeerb . . . Heeerb!" Calling for Herb, see, that's one of the many euphemisms for vomit. Others include spew, burp, hurl, the big spit, the long spit, throw, the whip o' will, the Technicolor laugh and, in Queensland, the chuckle.'

'You're about the greatest collector of useless information the world has ever seen,' I said.

'I must make up a yarn on that subject. Anyway, the Cooper's Creek champ is in the cubicle calling for Herb and the judge says: "He's not calling anyone; he's going for the big

80

spit and that's not allowed in Darwin, so he's disqualified." He yells out: "Do you hear that? You're disqualified," and out he walks.

'Crooked Bed McCracken waits till the Cooper's Creek Chunderer comes out and he can see the chunder flowing under the door, and this gives him an idea. So, when the Cooper's Creek champ comes out looking white about the gills, Crooked Bed says to him: "What do you do for a crust, mate?" "Well," says the Chunderer, "I did want to be a grog-guzzler and live on side bets, but they'll bar me here in Darwin just because I go for the big spit occasionally." Crooked Bed McCracken exclaims: "Do you call that a spit? Listen, mate, that's no spit, that's the greatest Technicolor yodel in history. You've missed your vocation." '

'Technicolor yodel, that's another one.'

'Yeh, old Crooked Bed was a man of original mind. He says: "Look at that chunder: every colour in the rainbow." The Chunderer has a look and he has to admit he'd done a pretty colourful job of it.

'Crooked Bed says to him: "How long have you been in the game?" The Chunderer tells him: "Well, I started very young and I've kept at it. The colour varies according to what I eat."

'Anyway, old Crooked Bed takes him back to the bar, buys him a drink and says: "It's like I told yer, mate, you've missed your vocation. You should become a professional chunderer and I'll be your manager on a fifty-fifty basis. And we start at the Darwin Show tomorrow." '

'This is about the most ridiculous story you've ever told in your whole life and it's disgusting into the bargain.'

'I'll knock off immediately, if you object.'

'Not on your life. I want to hear how it finishes. No offence meant. Have another drink.'

'Thanks. Crooked Bed McCracken got a lawyer to draw up a chunder-tight contract and they were in business. Crooked Bed set up a tent and put up a sign, "The Technicolor Yodeller—the first time in history—money back guarantee if he doesn't yodel in Technicolor." Well, the public rolled in, needless to say, and the Yodeller yodelled into a chunder bucket in full Technicolor (Crooked Bed McCracken had fed him on tucker of all different colours). The crowd groaned and went crook and complained (some of them had a quiet chuckle on the side), but they couldn't get their money back because the yodel was in Technicolor; that no one could deny.'

'Here's your beer. I can't stand much more of this.'

'Neither could the Darwin mob at the show. By the end of the first day, Crooked Bed had made $500 but someone went to the police and they closed the show up. But Crooked Bed never turned a hair. The Sydney Show was due to start and he had an idea. "Can you really yodel and sing?" he asks the Chunderer. "I used to be a pupil of Tex Morton—singing and yodelling and playing the Jew's harp." Crooked Bed throws his hat in the air. "You stick to yodelling and singing. I'll play the Jew's harp."

'So the old Crooked Bed writes a song called "The Happy Chunderer" to the tune of "The Happy Wanderer" and they opened at the Royal Easter Show in Sydney. The Chunderer sang, with Crooked Bed on the Jew's harp: "I am a happy chunderer. I chunder all day long, I chunder here, I chunder there . . ." then the "Ha, ha, ha" bit. At that point the Chunderer, suitably fed on colourful tucker, would yodel in Technicolor as advertised.'

'You're going from bad to worse.'

'If you don't believe me you can look up the minutes of the special meeting of the Royal Agricultural Society which met to consider the protest from the press and public. Needless to say, that narrer-minded Sydney mob disqualified the Chunderer and put Crooked Bed out of business.

'Next day, the Manly Surf Club, which numbers amongst its members some of the best chunderers in the southern hemisphere, issued a challenge for the Technicolor Yodeller to meet their champion, a young bloke named Chunderous Charlie, for a side bet of a thousand dollars. They were short of funds as usual and thought it would be picking up money. Chunderous Charlie had beaten the university champion only a week before. The conditions were that they drank a flagon of plonk laced with Chanel No. 5 perfume. On that monstrous mixture they considered Chunderous Charlie unbeatable.

'By the way, Chunderous Charlie was the bloke that Barry Humphries wrote the song about: you know, the one about chundering in the great Pacific sea.

'They went at it one night on the football oval opposite the RSL Club in Manly. A great crowd gathered. The judges laced the plonk with the perfume and away they went, chundering on gaily. It was the greatest exhibition of the chunder ever witnessed in the history of the human race. Each one sang his own theme song between the Technicolor yodels. Within an hour they'd filled the football oval until chunder was oozing through the picket fence. But before they could pick a winner, the coppers intervened and arrested the two of them for creating a public nuisance.'

'One of these days you'll be arrested on the same charge.'

'After the Yodeller came out of jail, the university champion, known simply as Herb's Mate, issued a challenge, but the police intervened and a new by-law was written forbidding chundering for commercial purposes.

'The old Crooked Bed was a bit upset, needless to say, but he was far from beaten. "Yodeller, me old chunderous mate," he says, "we ain't beat yet. There must be some way of honestly exploiting your unique talent."

'Well, they were driving up George Street at the time in Crooked Bed's old bomb. Crooked Bed got carried away with his thinking and ran into a fire hydrant. The hydrant burst and the Yodeller broke into a big chunder all over himself and his manager. They got out of the car and washed the chunder off under the gusher of water. "Let's get away from here," says Crooked Bed. "If the coppers catch us, we're goners." '

'I hope the coppers gave them ten years. Have another beer.'

'The coppers' car drove up that very moment. The Yodeller says to Crooked Bed: "I had cheese for tea; I think I can seal it." With that he let go a sharp chunder that sealed the fire hydrant just as the police pulled up. "It's the wrong colour," says Crooked Bed desperately. And the Yodeller ate a tomato he was carrying and flashed a chunder the exact red colour of the hydrant. The coppers had nothing on 'em, mate.'

'Here's your beer. Get it over with, for the love of all that's good and holy.'

'The incident with the fire hydrant gave old Crooked Bed the idea of the century. "The trick is, old mate," he says, "to think of something you can do at home where the coppers can't interfere, and we'll sell it afterwards." So they conferred far into the night. Perhaps they could use chunder instead of vulcanising or solder. No, too hard on the old Yodeller.

'Suddenly, in the middle of the night, Crooked Bed hit on the solution. "Why didn't I think of it in the first place?" he yelled. "Paintings, mate, abstract paintings. You paint me in full colour and we'll win the Archibald Prize." '

'I give up. Just have another drink and say no more about it.'

'And so it came to pass that the Technicolor Yodeller won the Archibald Prize with a portrait of that well-known business man and philanthropist, Crooked Bed McCracken, Esquire.'

'No more.'

'A'course, Crooked Bed had to feed him on various things to get the colours—tomatoes, Condy's crystals, penicillin tablets, rose petals, *et cetera*. But it was worth the trouble and expense. The Yodeller went on to win several painting prizes in America, one with a portrait of LBJ. The second prize went to a painting done by an orang-outang monkey with its tail.'

'I should know better by this time, but I'll ask the $64 question: What became of the Technicolor Yodeller?'

'Who? The Champion Chunderer from Cooper's Creek? Well, he met an untimely end. It was his great love of the Northern Territory that led to his death. Had the biggest funeral since Bill Harney. The Todd River was as dry as a bone, so the Yodeller guaranteed to end the drought. He flew up to the Alice with Crooked Bed, drank bore water for three days and nights, then chundered into the Todd River. He called for Herb the whole weekend and soon the Todd was in full flow.'

'Come on. How did he come to die?'

'Through Crooked Bed's greed. The whole town was there and a great cheer went up. "I'll bet a thousand dollars he can swim across the Todd," Crooked Bed yelled. Someone snapped up the bet and he pushed the Chunderer in. But he forgot to ask if he could swim. The Chunder sank midstream and was never seen or heard of again.'

'And good riddance to him. Just as well you've finished or I'd chunder myself.'

18

That Australian men have big dongers.

THE DEATH OF DOOLEY FRANKS

There I was in the Woolpack Inn, Parramatta, when Truthful Jones came in with a face as long as a wet week.

'What's wrong, Truthful,' I asked, 'you back a hundred-to-one winner and lose the ticket?'

Truthful tipped his hat on to the back of his head and began to actually shed a tear. 'I'm a man who bears sad, sad, tidings: Dooley Franks is dead!'

I felt a great sense of loss—and disbelief. 'Dooley Franks dead? I always thought he'd live forever . . .'

Truthful insisted. 'He's dead all right. I heard the rumour. Then I met Whynot Ronnie in the Pelican RSL near Newcastle. Ron was an old mate of Dooley's, as you know, and he confirmed the sad news. Dooley Franks is definitely dead.'

I bought drinks and we sipped, sadly silent, for once in our lives. Then Truthful said: 'He was a legend in his own lifetime . . . While the Australian battler battles Dooley Franks will never be forgotten.'

'He was a man who rode the wild bull through Wagga Wagga—backwards!' I said.

Truthful added, 'He dug the Murray River so Sturt could sail down it . . .'

'He backed the card twice in one year, once at Flemington and once at Randwick . . .' I remembered.

Truthful added, 'He threw seven heads at Thommo's Two-up school five times . . .'

'Yes, on the last occasion he won 5,000 lovely quid and decided to join the Tattersall's Club . . .' I recalled.

'Yeh,' Truthful said. 'How long ago did you write that yarn about him tryin' to join the Tattersall's Club and havin' to get the three references in person? Famous people, not Australians, and Dooley went with the secretary of the Tattersall's Club to Washington to see Eisenhower, to Moscow to see Khrushchev and to Rome to see the Pope.'

I laughed, 'Yeh, thirty years ago I wrote that and I still hear it told in pubs up and down the country, and my recording of it is occasionally played on the radio. The Yankee tourist couldn't recognise the Pope but he definitely recognised Dooley Franks from Parramatta . . .'

'Dooley he was brought up in Parramatta,' Truthful said. 'I went to school with Dooley here.'

I bought another round of drinks and sat pondering the nature of life and death and how some people are of the stuff that makes legends—like Dooley Franks. 'I didn't think they could have killed him with an axe. How did he die, Truthful?'

'Died in action, fell on the battlefield!' Truthful replied.

'What? Don't tell me Dooley became a mercenary and fought with the Contras or in some foreign war?'

'No, he died in the battle of the sexes, in action in the sack,' Truthful replied. 'If you don't believe me you can ask Whynot Ronnie. Ron told me the whole story of how Truthful died in the Townsville Hospital.

'It appears that, at the age of ninety, he had a heart attack in the middle of sexual intercourse with a thirty-year-old waitress. She rushed him to hospital . . . Ronnie reckons it must have been funny 'cos there's Dooley unconscious and they're tryin' to breathe life back into him, tried mouth-to-mouth resuscitation and every known treatment, but in the end old Dooley passed away to that great land beyond the skies where the Australian battlers reside.'

I asked Truthful: 'I thought you said it was funny! What could possibly be funny about the death of a legend like Dooley Franks?'

Truthful replied, emptying his glass, 'What was funny was he had an erection all through the period of unconsciousness and after he died . . .'

Truthful was in such a hurry to get on with the story that he bought a drink by accident. 'Y'know, Dooley Franks was the only legendary hero in Australia's history from Ned Kelly onwards who was even more popular with women than he was with men. Most heroes in this sexist society are men and they have men followers. But Dooley had even more fame amongst women than he did amongst men.'

'You don't tell,' I said. 'And what do you put that strange circumstance down to?'

'Well, accordin' to Whynot Ronnie, Dooley Franks had the biggest donger that ever grew on a human being. He was as well slung as a brewery horse. Did I tell you that he regained consciousness for three days . . .'

'No you didn't . . .'

'Well, he did and, as usual, he was very very popular with all the women—the nurses and sisters and visitors. And when he died the head doctor of the hospital came on his rounds to find a group of nurses and sisters wailin' and cryin': "Dooley Franks is dead!" one said, then another said "Yes, Dooley Franks is dead, it's a terrible thing!" and they all chanted together: "Oh sad sad day: Dooley Franks is dead."

'So this here head doctor says: "Come, now, sisters, why are you so upset by the death of Dooley Franks? You only knew him a few days. He was an old man. He wasn't rich, he wasn't famous, he wasn't handsome . . ."

'The nurses continued wailing and the head sister called the doctor aside and took him to the bed where Dooley Franks was lying dead and there stood the biggest donger in the southern hemisphere in full erection in the middle under the sheet: like a tentpole, so the bed itself looked like a tent . . .'

'Have another beer—and get on with the story!' I said, suiting my actions to the words.

Truthful continued: 'So this here doctor looks at the tent-pole and, when the sister went away, he lifted up the blanket and he thought "Wowee! What a donger! So that's why all the nurses and sisters are crying and lamenting the loss of Dooley Franks." So he thinks, "I'm gonna cut this donger off and take it home and show it to my missus. No one's gonna believe that such a magnificent instrument could exist unless they actually see it. Who knows, I might get it pickled and put some batteries on it, and use it as a vibrator."

'So he looks around for a newspaper to wrap Dooley Franks's donger in. First he tries the *Telegraph* and it's not big enough to cover it, then he tried the *Sun* and then the *Mirror*, but the papers weren't big enough to roll up Dooley's donger. So the doctor goes to his own office and he gets a copy of the *Sydney Morning Herald*, and he goes back to the hospital ward, saws off Dooley's donger and found that the *Herald* would just wrap around it . . .'

I rubbed my chin doubtfully.

'This story's spot on true,' Truthful said. 'Whynot Ronnie is a man who treats the truth with great respect—and this is what he told me. Well, the doctor wrapped up Dooley's donger in the *Herald* and that evening he went home and put it on the kitchen table still wrapped up. He thought: "I'll clean it up a bit and show the missus." With that the telephone rang and he went to answer it. As he came back towards the kitchen door he heard his wife wailing and crying: "Dooley Franks is dead! Dooley Franks is dead!"

'The doctor got quite a shock at his wife crying and lamenting just like the nurses at the hospital. And she goes on: "Dooley Franks is dead!"

'And the doctor asked: "How do you know?"

'And his wife replied: "I saw it in the *Herald*!" '

After a pause for laughter, I threatened, 'Truthful, one day I swear I'll kill you in the middle of one of your yarns.'

Truthful grinned. 'The last words of Dooley Franks were: Enjoy yourself, it's longer than you think.'

19

That Aborigines have a different attitude to democracy.

DEMOCRACY HAS TO WORK BOTH WAYS

I was reading a newspaper in the Harold Park Hotel when who should walk in but Truthful Jones, and I said: 'I see in the paper here, Truthful, where —'

'Ah, you don't want to believe everything you read in the papers. The press is not free in this country. You try to start a daily newspaper; see how much money you need.'

'Well, the press is not free in Russia either, let's admit it.'

'I'm not talking about Russia. In the West journalists write things that don't happen; in the East journalists do not write things that do happen.'

'It's getting a bit complicated. Have a drink.'

'I'll force this one down just to be sociable. Democracy never works both ways, that's the trouble. It's always one-way traffic. Only the Aborigines know how to make democracy work both ways. Did I ever tell you about what happened on a cattle station in the Northern Territory when they tried to register the natives for voting?'

'Here's your beer. This is where the Aborigines got equal rights, years ago?'

'Equal rights! They got the right to get rotten drunk like

you and me, but not enough dough to buy the grog with.'

'So you're one of those who reckon the Aborigines will waste their money on grog if they get equal pay.'

'I never said that. I said that all they got was the right to get drunk in pubs and the right to vote. They don't get enough money to be democratic. On the cattle stations they work for six dollars a week and keep. They're equal in everything except money and that means they're not equal at all, like women, but they know how to make democracy work both ways.'

'Their tribal laws are not democratic,' I argued. 'The elders have all the power and no-one can vote.'

'All you can think of is voting. The Aborigine will share and share alike with his relatives and that's more democratic than voting. The tribal law says he must share all, and he does— even his money—and good luck to him, I say. He can make democracy work both ways.

'Yer see, there was this here electoral officer and they sent him out on the cattle stations down the track to register Aboriginal voters. Anyway, he gets to this station right out along the Victoria River somewhere and gets talkin' to some young Aboriginal ringers about registering to vote. They seem quite happy about it, but say they have to ask the elders of the tribe.'

'What did I tell you,' I exclaimed. 'That's not democratic.'

'Don't get upset. These young ringers go and ask the elder of the tribe, an old bloke with white hair and a wrinkled face, smoking a pipe made from the claw of a crab. And they try to explain to him about registering to vote, and voting in order of preference for the two candidates at the forthcoming elections for the NT Legislative Council. He listens, puzzled, and asks them a lot of questions in their own lingo, and they ask this white electoral officer and translate for him. The old bloke looks more puzzled than ever; then he consults with the other elders of the tribe. They yak-yak away in the Gurindji language and at last they say: "No, us mob no vote belonga them white fellas in Darwin. They tell us vote for two white fella. Maybe them two white fellas no good for us native people. No savvy this voting for two white fellas." '

'The electoral officer should have explained that they vote for whichever they think is the best.'

'He did, but the old Aborigine said: "Maybe both bad men. Maybe one of them that fella belonga Brisbane Joh." That's something the average white fella never thinks when he talks about democracy: he has no say in the candidates who are going to stand.

'Anyway, this electoral officer argues the toss for an hour with this old bloke, then says they will get fined $25 each if they don't register and vote. Everyone over twenty-one in the tribe will get fined if he don't vote. So they explain this to the elder of the tribe, and he says: "You bin tellin' me we all pay nearly week's money just *not* to vote for two white fellas. That right?" "That's bloody right," says the electoral officer, sick of the argument by this time.'

'What did the old fella say to that?'

'After long yak-yak with the other elders of the tribe he says. "The white fellas up Darwin not worth $25, so we vote for them. We bin thinkin' that cheaper." So the electoral officer registers the whole lot after taking about six hours to get all their names right and get their thumbmarks on the forms. Nobody bothered to teach them to read or write out on the stations—only to muster, brand and inject cattle, and to vote.'

'How did they get on with their first vote?'

'Never turned a hair. Some voted for both candidates, some voted for neither by mucking up their ticket. Then a smart-Alec candidate visited them and told them to vote for his opponent: "Him bin good fella; give him two votes and me only one vote." Then the other candidate got hold of their tickets and changed them so they all voted for him. But they didn't know and they wouldn't have cared if they did know because it made no difference to them who won; they still worked long hours for six dollars a week, bread and salt beef, or were unemployed.

'Anyway, this here electoral officer gives a statement to the papers how well the natives understood democracy and everybody is happy because the Aborigines are equal just like us and they vote and don't cause any trouble or answer back to white men, or anything undemocratic like that, or ask for equal pay.

'Next month the winning candidate dies, see, and there's a by-election to replace him. So word gets around the native camp about the voting coming on again like the wet season or foot-rot in the cattle. So up they go, led by the elder of the tribe, to the homestead and ask the book-keeper for the papers to vote. "Doesn't matter which one," the elder says, "just so long we don't bin fined." But it turns out there's only one candidate: the bloke who had stood before and got beat. So the station book-keeper tries to explain this and the elder consults his mates and he says: "Well, in that case, we bin vote for that white fella with name on that paper." But the book-keeper says: "There's no need to because this man wins without any votes." Well, the elder of the tribe yak-yaks away to his mates and then he asks: "You got no vote belonga us this time, boss?" "That's right, no vote belonga you this time," says the book-keeper, glad to be rid of them for a lot of black nuisances.

'One day, that there electoral officer is sitting in his office when who should walk in but a few members of the Gurindji tribe. "What can I do for you?" says the electoral officer, who's very proud that he had taught this tribe all about democracy.'

'And what did the old fella say?'

'He says, "I bin come along to get $25 each belonga my mob." "How do you mean?" says the electoral officer. "I don't owe you any money." And the elder of the tribe replied: "'You been owin' all my mob $25. Last time you bin tell us we have to pay if we bin not voting. This time you bin not let us vote. That vote him worth $25. You pay 'em now, boss?"

I couldn't help roaring with laughter. 'Votes at twenty-five bucks a throw!'

'The Aborigines have forgotten more about democracy than we'll ever learn.' Truthful concluded, 'They know that democracy has to work both ways.'

20

That greed and revenge are a terrible mixture.

HOW CROOKED BED McCRACKEN MADE THE WRONG MIXTURE

'How are you, Truthful?' I asked, in the Harold Park Hotel.

'Not bad meself, but I'm worried about a mate of mine. A con man sold him some brummy oil shares; promised he'd clean up a quick fortune. But the shares turned out to be worthless. Now my mate is trying to find who the con man is, to take his revenge on him.'

'Don't blame him.'

'What? It was his own fault. If he hadn't been so greedy, he wouldn't have fallen for the trick. These con men work on people's greed. You can't con an honest man. Now he wants revenge and, believe me, greed and revenge are a terrible mixture.'

'Sounds like another myth. Have a glass and get on with it.'

'Don't mind if I do. Yes, greed and revenge are a terrible mixture, as old Crooked Bed McCracken always said to his dying day.'

'Crooked Bed. Why call a man a name like that?'

'Simple reason: he was so crooked he couldn't lay straight in bed. They reckon he had to get a special crooked bed made to sleep in. He was greedy—(which is bad enough 'cos greed causes most of the troubles in the world, such as hire-purchase debts, gambling, wars and stock-exchange jobbery)—but when you mix revenge with greed then you've really got trouble.'

'Here's your beer. I don't see the point.'

'Crooked Bed could see the point after what happened to him in North Queensland during the thirties depression. Crooked Bed was as free of fivers as a frog is of feathers. Used to work around the country shows with some racket or another, usually a sideshow. You know the kind of thing—a shy stall, a merry-go-round or a flea circus. Reckoned there was a mug born every minute. Had exhibited pygmies, half-men, half-women, a man with two heads, a three-legged dog and a mother-in-law with a happy nature. But when the depression hit him he lost all his capital and had nothing to exhibit. There he is with a mate in a country pub, spending

his last shilling on beer, trying to think of something to exhibit at the local show. They've run out of ideas when Crooked Bed drains his glass and says: "Old mate, shake hands with a genius: I've just thought of the greatest idea in history. We'll exhibit the Wild Man from Borneo."

'But his mate wasn't impressed; simple sort of fellow, wanted to know how they could get to Borneo to find the Wild Man. But old Crooked Bed says: "The Wild Man from Borneo is right here in this bar." His mate looked around but he can't see any wild man. "Look in the mirror," Crooked Bed tells him. But his mate suddenly remembered the last time Crooked Bed had exhibited a Wild Man from Borneo, chained by the neck to an iron peg in a hole eight feet deep. "Not on your life," he tells Crooked Bed. "You're not throwing soup bones to me in a hole at feeding time. Tell you what: you be the Wild Man from Borneo and I'll throw the bones to you."

'Needless to say Crooked Bed couldn't agree to such a proposition, seeing he was a natural-born foreman and employer of labour, only being short of the wherewithal to indulge his taste for being a boss. Well, they were having a dry argument about who would become the Wild Man from Borneo, when a stranger walks into the bar. And talking about dry arguments . . .'

'I can take a hint. Have another beer. The plot thickens but I can't see what it's got to do with greed and revenge.'

'Well, the greed was them wanting to rob the public and the revenge part had just walked into the bar. Crooked Bed's mate slews on to this stranger. "Listen, mate," he says to Crooked Bed, "am I seeing things or is that the warder from the military boob in Syria who stood over us for three months during the war?" Crooked Bed studies this character. "It can't be. I've waited nearly fifteen years to meet up with him—it is him! He walks right into the pub, into me loving arms." His mate says: "He's big and ugly enough to beat the two of us. What'll wc do to him? Perhaps we could slip some thallium into his beer when he ain't lookin'." But Crooked Bed says no—couldn't let him die a painless death. His mate keeps making suggestions like burning the ex-warder's house down, but Crooked Bed doesn't turn a hair. His mate gets upset. "Remember what he did to us in military prison," he says. "Pack drill at the double, running up and down for hours, cleaning our cells with toothbrushes, solitary confinement on bread and water. Tell you what we'll do: we'll wait till he goes for a Jerry Riddle, foller him, knock him down from behind, take all his money, lock him in the back bar and make him do all the things he did to us, while we watch him and drink beer." '

'I'm sure that suggestion would appeal to the delicate nature of Crooked Bed McCracken,' I said with relish.

'His mate thought it would but Crooked Bed had other ideas to mix greed with revenge. So he says: "Take a look at the head on the monster, like a diseased poultice hanging over a hospital balcony. With about three days' growth on and that hairy chest and pot belly, he'd be the dead-set replica of the Wild Man from Borneo. Follow me, old mate; revenge is sweet. He's a mug from way back, hasn't got enough brains to give hisself a headache. We'll interest him in a slight business proposition." '

'Here's your beer. Did the warder recognise them?'

'Didn't have to. Crooked Bed fronts him and says: "Pardon me intruding, old chap, but were you a warder in the Australian military prison in Syria during the war?" The ex-warder snarls and says: "I was and what are you going to do about it?" "Nothing," says Crooked Bed. "Just that my mate here and me was in your tender care for an all-too-brief sojourn and we just want to thank you for the many kindnesses you showed us." The ex-warder couldn't believe his ears. "Well, that's mighty fine of you," he says. "I always tried to act according to regulations, to be fair, but firm." "How very true," says Crooked Bed. "Fair but firm is the only way to describe it. Me and me mate have never looked back since, due to the way you taught us the error of our ways and reformed us on the path of virtue." '

'The dumb warder is still a bit suspicious, see. "Every prisoner I've met since has wanted to fight me. I'll admit there were times when I might have been a bit hard, but it was for the prisoners' good." Crooked Bed winks at his mate. "Just take a look at me and me mate, living examples of the efficacy of your methods. And we'd like to make some small repayment for your help and kindness. What would you be doing these days? In the police force, maybe, or the Prisons Department?" The ex-warder says: "I'm unemployed through no fault of me own. I was framed; I joined the force and they kicked me out just because I fell on a criminal and ruptured his kidneys; it was an accident." Crooked Bed clucked his tongue: "Ah, the injustice of the world. But a friend in need is a friend indeed. Would you have anything left out of your life's savings? We have a proposition, strictly business: we put in a hundred pounds each and . . ." The ex-warder interrupts him: "I've only got a fiver between me and starvation." "Well, a fiver each . . . Tell you what we'll do . . ." '

'Don't tell me the warder fell for it.'

'Old Crooked Bed was the best magsman in Australia—with the exception of Don't tell a Soul, the Sydney urger. He bull-dusted and yak-yakked while the ex-warder paid for the beer and finally agreed to hand over his fiver and play the part of the Wild Man from Borneo, the profits to be split three ways. Crooked Bed goes down to the store and buys some hessian and five iron stakes. And after the ex-warder had grown a wiry beard and dug a hole eight feet deep out at the showgrounds, they were in business.'

'Surely the public wouldn't pay to look at a Wild Man from Borneo,' I said.

'The public are like sheep as soon as they walk on to a fairground—ready to be shorn. Crooked Bed rigged the hessian around the four stakes, drove the fifth stake into the bottom of the hole and chained the Wild Man from Borneo to it by the neck. The Wild Man looked fierce with his beard and hairy chest, and Crooked Bed had rolled him in dirt, in the interests of realism. He wore only a loin cloth. "Roll up! Roll up!" Crooked Bed spruiked to the crowd on opening day. "It's feeding time for the Wild Man from Borneo. The only one in captivity, direct from the jungles of Borneo at great expense. Roll up!" Well, the crowd rolls in and there they see the Wild Man from Borneo himself, at the bottom of the deep hole, grunting and growling and scratching his chest (the warder turned out to be a born actor under Crooked Bed's expert tuition). Crooked Bed's mate tossed the Wild Man from Borneo a bone occasionally and he grabbed it and chewed it.'

'He must have been an actor and no mistake. Have another drink. This is the best story you've told for a long time; can't wait to hear the end of it.'

'Barley Charley, the detail is important. The Wild Man wasn't acting when he ate the meat off the bones; that was all the tucker Crooked Bed gave him for the whole week; reckoned the public might get wise if anyone saw the hole empty, so that Wild Man had to stay there day and night. Stinking hot days and cold nights. Like being in solitary confinement, Crooked Bed reckoned. And his diet was water and soup bones.

'Anyway, they made a clear profit of 300 quid in the week of the show. When the show finished, Crooked Bed and his mate counted the money. "Three hundred quid," his mate tells Crooked Bed. "That's a hundred quid each for the three of us." Crooked Bed gets upset. "Have you taken leave of your senses, mate? Have you forgotten who the Wild Man from Borneo is? He gets nothing, which means 150 quid each for us, who deserve every penny of it."

'Crooked Bed's mate, who was a bit soft-hearted, asks: "What will we do with him?" Crooked Bed snorts: "Leave the bludger there." His mate is worried, see. "The coppers might find him." "Then, let 'em send him back to Borneo where he belongs," says Crooked Bed. And off they chooff into town to buy an old truck and hit the road.'

'A terrible mixture, all right, greed and revenge.'

Truthful sipped his beer. 'You can say that again. That evening, the workers cleaning up the showgrounds hear the Wild Man grunting and groaning—and he's not putting on an act any more—so they send for the lollipops. The local sergeant had been trying to get something on Crooked Bed for years, so he gives chase in a new police car and arrests Crooked Bed and his mate. Charged them with conspiracy, fraud, untruthful advertising, cruelty, obstructing a police officer in the course of duty, offensive behaviour and using obscene language. They got fined 150 quid each and six months' jail. It's like you said, mate, greed and revenge are a terrible mixture.'

That cheats never prosper—if they've got principles.

HOW PRINCIPLES BROUGHT CROOKED BED UNDONE

'A terrible mixture all right, Truthful?' I said in the Bilinud-gel Hotel.

'What? This beer? Be your age; it's not as good a drink as you'll get anywhere in the world—and I ought to know; I've drunk more beer than a brewery taster.'

'I don't mean the beer, I mean that story you told me a few days ago about the Wild Man from Borneo. Greed and revenge are a terrible mixture and no mistake, after what that fellow did. What was his name again?'

'Crooked Bed McCracken. Ah, old Crooked Bed wasn't a bad fella when you got to know him. His trouble was he always stuck to his principles.'

'Funny sort of principles: leaving a man chained to a stake by the neck in an eight-foot hole . . .'

'The principle he worked on there was, never give a sucker an even break. But I never had time to finish the story before the pub shut.'

'Why didn't you finish it outside?'

'Can't tell a story without a glass of beer in me hand.'

'Well, I'll put one in your hand right now. Why is it, Truthful, there are more con men and scams in Australia than anywhere in the world!'

'Well, my father reckoned it was because of our convict origins: we whinge about the injustice of the system but never raise a hand against it: we'd rather fiddle around the rules. Scratch your average Australian and you'll find a con.' Truthful Jones tiltled his hat back and continued.

'Old Crooked Bed and his mate go to jail and, with remissions for good behaviour, they're out in four months. Old Crooked Bed decides to go straight, to change his principles. He decides he'll never be greedy or seek revenge, and he'll never impose on anyone who does the right thing by him. First of all he tells his mate: "It's a mug's game, going to jail. We'll get out of the rackets and set ourselves up in an honest business." His mate was a simple soul, like I told yer. He says: "But I thought you always said all businesses is crook, banks and shops and all that. Only crooks with a licence, you always reckoned." Old Crooked Bed was determined. "With us it'll be different." So they set themselves up as ranchers.'

'Here's your beer. Ranchers? Where would they get the money to buy a ranch?'

Truthful sipped reflectively. 'In North Queensland a rancher is a bloke who runs a sort of boarding house out in the bush, near some big job. Rigs up a cookhouse and a few tents, charges so much for each bed and so much for a feed. Now, old Crooked Bed McCracken knew a storekeeper in a town in the North who was the only man in Australia who would give him credit. Crooked Bed had saved his kid from drowning, which didn't cost him anything. So they head for this town, see, and the storekeeper welcomes Crooked Bed with open arms and gives him hundreds of quids' worth of credit. This storekeeper's name was Honest John Jackson, the only truly honest man who was ever born in Queensland; was so honest he never even cheated on his tax returns.'

'Must have been honest and no mistake,' I laughed.

'They didn't call him Honest John for nothing. Anyway, Crooked Bed and his mate are in business and Crooked Bed is determined to stick to his new principles. "And we'll do the right thing by Honest John; pay him back every penny and settle our monthly bills dead on the knocker."

'Well, the road to hell is paved with good intentions, as they say in the classics. Things went all right at the ranch for a while, but pretty soon their debt at the store got bigger instead of smaller. Trouble was Crooked Bed had become too honest, too much of a man of principle. His tucker was the best and dirt cheap. He insisted on putting sheets on the beds and white cloths on the tables. A lot of his customers had put money on the slate and shot through without paying. The bad debts were his main trouble, so his mate says one day: "Listen, Crooked, old mate, why don't we stand over some of these blokes who aren't paying, give 'em a bit of a kicking to remind them of their responsibilities?" Old Crooked Bed was upset. "Mate," he says, "how could you suggest such a thing! Seeking revenge is against my principles. Look where it got us last time." His mate says: "Well, why don't we jack the prices up to allow for the bad debts?" "Never let it be said that Crooked Bed McCracken would act from motives of greed," was the reply. "Well then, let us do a moonlight flit and leave old Honest John for dead. It's our only hope," says his mate. But Old Crooked Bed wouldn't hear of the moonlight flit idea. "I'll pay Honest John if it's the last thing I do," he says.

'But things went from bad to worse. Their credit was still good with Honest John, but they were losing money hand over fist, money they never had. Then, one day, Crooked Bed's mate was riding home from the town when he sees a thoroughbred racehorse roaming unattended in the bush. So he leads it home to Crooked Bed, and he says: "Crooked, old mate, you always said you would make a fortune if you had a good racehorse. Well, I got one for yer, and we'll win the local cup with it next month."

'Well, Crooked Bed knew a good horse when he saw one. "It's a good horse and no mistake; there's nothing around here would beat it." Turned out that this horse was a ring-in from the south. The smarties who brought it up had hunted it into the bush after they won a race with it, so's to get rid of the evidence. Anyway, old Crooked Bed altered its brand and markings and started to train it for the cup.

'Hey, wait a minute,' I interjected. 'Thought you said Crooked Bed McCracken had new principles, never to be greedy and so on. Here's your beer. How do you explain that?'

'Easy! Old Crooked Bed lay awake nights worrying about what he was planning to do and he works it out that to keep one principle you have to break another. If he was going to pay Honest John who had done the right thing by him he'd have to be greedy just once more. So they get this horse fighting fit, ready to run the race of its life. They timed it to run three furlongs in thirty-eight seconds on a dirt track. A'course, they were timing it with an alarm clock but that was still good time. Then they timed the other runner in the cup. No chance of their horse getting beat. Now, the first prize for the cup was a hundred quid, but they owed Honest John, the storekeeper, four hundred. "Well, our horse is five-to-one," says Crooked Bed's mate. "We can have a hundred quid on it, pay the storekeeper and have 200 nicker left for ourselves," which was good mathematics, whatever way you look at it, as Crooked Bed was forced to admit. "A'course," he says, "there is the small matter of where we're going to get a hundred quid." His mate had a ready answer: "Borrow it from the storekeeper. After all, we're only doing this for Honest John, and this way he gets his hundred back and the four hundred we owe him chucked in." '

'Don't tell me Honest John Jackson loaned Crooked Bed McCracken another hundred pounds to back a racehorse!'

'Without hesitation. After all, Crooked Bed had saved his kid from drowning and was a man of new principles who had only ventured into the sport of kings in order to pay Honest John his due accounts. So they get the hundred quid off Honest John.'

'I know: they put it on the horse: it won, and they lived happily ever after.'

'As luck would have it, before they could get the bet on, a dark horse arrived from Brisbane to be trained for the cup, so Crooked Bed decides to time it in a training gallop before he backs his own horse, see. He hides behind a tree at daylight and times the gallop, and this horse runs three in thirty-six on the bit. Well, you can imagine how old Crooked Bed felt, having broken his principles for no good purpose.

'So he goes to see the trainer-owner-rider of the dark horse from the south, a little bloke with sandy hair and a white-handled pocket knife. "Run your horse dead and back mine," he urges the little bloke. But the little bloke only laughs at Crooked Bed. "Listen," he says, "that there horse of yours couldn't win a two-horse race, if the other was a Shetland pony."

'So, Crooked Bed and his mate have a conference. His mate says: "Why don't we nobble his horse—that'll teach him—or maybe hunt it into the bush at the barrier?" "That would be dishonest," Crooked Bed tells him. "And, anyway, I've got a better idea. His horse is six-to-one. We'll back it instead of our own; same results." '

'A man of principle, and that's for sure,' I said.

'A victim of circumstances, like the rest of us,' Truthful defended.

'Well, at least Honest John got paid.'

'It was a funny thing. Before they backed the little bloke's horse, Crooked Bed's mate suggested that they see the judge and get him to give the race to their horse if it ran second.'

'Some of those country judges would do it, too, if you ask me. Who was the judge?'

'Honest John, the storekeeper.'

'No use asking him.'

'Crooked Bed wouldn't do it, anyway. So they put their hundred quid on the little bloke's horse and stand to get out of debt with a bit to spare. Crooked Bed tells his jockey not to win, just in case. "Run second," he says. "The second prize will come in handy. But don't make it too close; these country judges have got bad eyesight." So it turns out that the horse from Brisbane wins by three-quarters of a length, with Crooked Bed's horse second. Crooked Bed picks up his hat and says to his mate: "Come on, let us collect our bet, pay Honest John and get out of the district before they wake up to what we've done."

'They're just hurrying into the betting ring when Crooked Bed's mate grabs him by the arm. "What number's our horse?" "Two. It ran second." His mate says: "The judge has put its number up first. Listen to the crowd booing." Crooked Bed rushes over to the judge's box. Honest John is just stepping down. Crooked Bed says to him: "My horse got beat by nearly a length," and Honest John Jackson looks over his shoulder and whispers: "I know, but I realised how much it meant to you. The bloke who brought the winner up here is a crook. It'll be on my conscience for the rest of me life, but I just couldn't let you down. The first dishonest thing I've ever done in me life, but it was worth it to see you out of debt and on your feet again." '

'Poor Old Crooked Bed.' I shed a crocodile tear. 'Won the race and only finished square. I can almost feel sorry for him. Have another drink. What became of him and his mate?'

'Well, they had to do a moonlight flit out of the district, for a start. They went back into the sideshow business. Last I heard of them, they were exhibiting a Wild Man from Borneo down at the Wyndham Show.'

'And who played the part of the Wild Man?' I asked.

'The little bloke with the sandy hair and the white-handled pocket knife who rode the actual winner of that cup race.' Truthful Jones sighed. 'To be a man of principle is a difficult thing.'

22

That punishment is not the way to stop crime.

HOW NOT GUILTY NELSON TOOK PUNISHMENT AWAY FROM CRIME

'I see in the paper here, where a bank clerk got five years for stealing money,' I said glancing out of the side of my paper.

'A pretty stiff sentence. What did he spend it on?' Truthful asked.

'Well, it says here he lost the money gambling.'

'The usual story. Every time you read about a man stealing from the firm he works for, it always comes out that he lost it gambling. If you punished people for gambling we'd all be in jail; there's no difference between gambling with your own money and with other people's, when you come to think of it. Banks gamble with other people's money, when you look at it right, and so do stockbrokers. Anyway, I always say that punishment is not the way to stop crime.'

'A'course, you'd be one of those do-gooders who think we should let prisoners out of jail each day to work on award wages or go home at weekends to sleep with their wives,' I said sarcastically.

'I'm a penal reformer, mate, and I don't care who knows it. There but for the grace of God go I; that's what I always say. This bank clerk was a bit unlucky, that's all. He borrows a few quid from the till to pay a bookmaker, loses again, then borrows a bit more trying to win it back and before he knows where he is, he owes the bank 10,000. Who's guilty, mate: him or the bookies or the government who run the tote he bet the money on? Ask yourself a few questions, mate.'

'You're in an argumentative mood today; you better have a beer and calm down.'

'I'll force one down just to be sociable.'

I chiacked Truthful. 'Come on now, what would you do to this bank clerk who would have gone on stealing for the rest of his life, if he hadn't been caught?'

'Well, a'course, it's hard to say when you put it like that. All I know is, punishment never reformed a man in history. It's the same all over the world. The powers that be believe in punishment but the jails get bigger and fuller, which goes to prove that punishment doesn't stop crime.'

'Some people get punished who are found not guilty,' I admitted. 'The remand yards of our jails are full—and some of those people will be acquitted, just because they had no bail money . . .'

Truthful rubbed his chin. 'Well, for openers, bail should be set according to the income of the accused, instead of the gravity of the crime . . .'

'The law is impartial,' I replied. 'A millionaire would get the same bail as a person on the dole. You remember that quote I got from Anatole France: "The Law in its majestic impartiality forbids alike the millionaire and the pauper to steal bread and sleep under bridges . . ." '

Truthful said, 'That sums it up.'

'Here's your beer. Seriously, with this bank clerk in the paper: what would you do with him?'

'Well, old Not Guilty Nelson, the shooftiest solicitor Sydney ever saw in all its legal history, solved a similar case one time to everyone's satisfaction.'

'Why did they call him Not Guilty?'

'Because he would never let his clients plead guilty, that's why. And he once defended a bank clerk who stole 10,000 quid. It's a true story which proves that punishment is not the way to stop crime. Anyway, this particular bloke I'm telling you about lay awake at night wondering what to do. He'd gambled away the money in less than a year and knew he would only get further in if he kept betting. So after lying awake every night for a month and biting his fingernails down to the quick, he decides to give himself up.'

I said mockingly: 'The only sensible thing to do: take his punishment like a man.'

'So he decides to consult a lawyer—had great faith in lawyers, for some reason—and get this lawyer to tell the bank that he'd pinched the money, then defend him in court. So he goes to see Not Guilty Nelson.'

'How could Not Guilty Nelson plead not guilty on his behalf when he admitted to stealing the money?'

'Wait till I tell yer. He goes into Not Guilty Nelson's office in the city and waits in the queue, nervous as if he was at the dentist's. Eventually, his turn comes. Not Guilty greets him warmly: "Don't look so glum, my friend, your case is in good hands. Tell me all about it." Well, the bank clerk stammers and stutters and tells what he's done and asks the lawyer to tell the bank. "Just a minute," says Not Guilty Nelson. "I've never pleaded guilty in me life." And the bank clerk says: "What? Have you been up yourself from time to time?" Not Guilty glares at him. "Of course I haven't. I meant I never plead guilty for my clients. It's a bad habit to get into. But before we go any further, have you got any money left?" The bank clerk admits he hasn't got a penny left, having given it all to bookmakers and the TAB. "What?" says Not Guilty. "Well, it's no use coming here if you've got no money. My time is valuable; get out."

'Well, the bank clerk is very upset. "But," he says, "they told me you were the best lawyer in Sydney." "So I am," admits Not Guilty. Just as the bank clerk is slinking out the door, Not Guilty Nelson calls after him: "Here, just a minute! Come back here. Do you think you could steal another 10,000 before they catch you?" Well, the young bank clerk gets the shock of his life: "What good would that do?" "Well," says Not Guilty, encouragingly, "you might as well be hung for a sheep as a lamb." "I won't get hung, will I?" Old Not Guilty's getting warmed up: "Not if you can steal another 10,000 bucks."

' "Can you steal another ten thousand?" insists Not Guilty. "Just answer me yes or no." "Well," says the bank clerk, "It's easy enough when you know how. Just a matter of suppressing a credit receipt or making out a false receipt for a bond deposit. Nothing to it, really." So old Not Guilty Nelson comes around the table and puts his arm on the kid's shoulder like a long-lost father. "Get another 10,000 and you won't have a worry in the world."

'So away choofs the bank clerk and blow me down if he doesn't come back the next week with 10,000 bucks and plonk it on Not Guilty's table. Nelson divides the money into two heaps of 5,000. "Now, 4,000 is for my fee, and you keep a thousand for yourself. The other 5,000 goes back to the bank." The bank clerk nearly collapses at his feet. "I don't understand," he says. Old Not Guilty slaps his back. "If people understood, they wouldn't have to consult lawyers. Now, you and I are going down to see the bank manager and give him back this 5,000. I've checked your record: nothing against you; excellent record; highly thought of at the bank; regular attender at church; in fact, butter wouldn't melt in your mouth—until you took up punting." '

'Don't tell me . . .'

'I'll tell you, all right, if you'll buy me another beer. So off they choof down to the bank and old Not Guilty weeps on the bank manager's shoulder about the sorrow the whole thing would cause the kid's mother (he never said anything about the likely reaction at Head Office, a'course) and said what a kind-hearted man he'd heard the manager was, and how the clerk was determined to make good the money and reform. "In fact," says Not Guilty, "I feel so confident in the boy's future that I am prepared to make good some of the money stolen, that is, $5,000—and here it is."

'And did the bank accept?'

'What else could they do? This way they avoided a scandal and got some of their money back on the knocker.'

'Bet it took them a long while to get the other balance.'

'Not so long. The kid got let off on a bond to be of good behaviour for ten years and never to gamble again. So, on Not Guilty Nelson's advice, he went on the stock exchange with the thousand he'd salvaged from the wreck. He's one of Sydney's best-respected stockbrokers today—and still gambling with other people's money.'

'As I've said before and, no doubt, I'll say again: I believe you but thousands wouldn't.'

'It's like I told yer. Punishment is not the way to stop crime.'

23

That They won't give the battler a fair go.

THEY ARE THE TROUBLE

Truthful Jones emptied his glass and said reflectively: 'You were probably right when you say that the basis of Australian humour is you can't win but you've got to battle . . .'

I ordered two more beers and nibbled on a Billinudgel pie. 'I thought you would agree; most of your stories are about battlers.'

'Yeh,' said Truthful, grabbing his glass in his great right hand. 'But the question is, who do the battlers battle against?'

He had me there. 'That's a good question . . . the government? . . . the system? . . .'

'*They*!' Truthful replied. 'That's who we have to battle against.'

'*They*?'

'*They*! Those bastards up there who won't give the battler a fair go.'

'Who are *they*?' I asked, and lined up another drink so as not to interrupt Truthful's flow.

'I've been trying to find out who *they* are for years—and I'm still working on it. Take the races. In Brisbane a few weeks ago, I was going to back Lord Ballina, see, and a fella comes up to me for no reason at all—I'd never seen him before in my life—yet he comes up and says: "*They* tell me Princess Tiber can't get beat. Just a matter of how far, *they* say."

'So I says: "*They* do, do *they*? I'd better back it, then." Needless to say, Lord Ballina beat Princess Tiber. So I see this character at the bar, see, so I goes over and says: "I thought you said *they* said Princess Tiber couldn't get beat."

' "So *they* did," he says. "And who were *they*?" I asks. And he didn't know who *they* were either. And he says to me: "I'm sorry mate, but it was their fault. *They* are the trouble." '

I said to Truthful: '*They* are the trouble. A good theme, that.'

'*They*'ve got a lot to answer for, all right,' Truthful continued. '*They* throw heads when you back tails at the two-up. *They* run their horses dead. *They* rob you in the parliament. *They* charge high rent. *They* start depressions. *They* cause wars. What *they* do is bad enough but why can't *they* ever learn?

'*They*'ll never learn. *They* wouldn't wake up if an Adelaide River dunny fell on 'em. They wouldn't know horse dung from clay unless they tasted it. They can't see any further than their noses. The more money *they* make, the less tax *they* pay. *They*'re sending the country broke. *They* say we've never had it so good. *They* say there's no such thing as a free lunch—but *they* eat one nearly every day. *They* won't give a man a fair go. *They* sell the country out to the Yanks. *They* couldn't run a raffle, mate, that's for sure!'

'*They* say it's a good idea to drown your sorrows,' I quipped, 'so you'd better have another beer.'

'*They* wouldn't know, mate. But I'll force one down just to be sociable. *They* start a lot of gossip, too. *They* say he married her for her money. *They* say she had to get married. *They* say their marriage is on the rocks. *They* say he's a bad payer. *They* say she's a smack addict.'

I warmed to Truthful's theme. 'What about the tax summit? Were *they* behind that?'

'No worries. *They* and no other, Keating promised to become Robin Hood and tax the rich and give it to the poor. Instead he became a dray driver and robbed the poor and gave it to the rich.'

I asked: 'Did *they* build the cart for him?'

Truthful replied: '*They* did indeed but *they*'re lousy carpenters. Trouble is: *they*'ve got other options. When the wheels came off the cart, *they* made a deal with Keating and Hawke for a worse tax package.'

Truthful Jones sighed, tipped his hat back with his thumb and gazed at the surrounding green-wooded hills of the Tweed Valley. '*They* are the trouble, all right . . .'

I sighed and lit my pipe. 'I wish we could find out who *they* are.'

'If wishes were Mercedes, beggars would ride in style,' Truthful replied. 'Next time someone sidles up to me and says: "*They* tell me the Opera House is going to be raffled," I'll say: "And who are *they*?" '

'Trouble is they won't know who *they* are,' I ventured.

'There you go, trying to spoil my story again. My father always said: "*They* will try to make you get ahead of your story, but don't let them." Every time anyone says: "*They* say . . ." I'll demand to know who *they* are.'

'But *they* won't tell you,' I chiacked him.

'Or maybe *they* wouldn't even know, as you say. But I'll work on it until I find out who *they* are. I've made up my mind to kill the lot of them.'

'Good idea,' I said. 'Have another beer before *they* close the pub.'

'Yeh, *they*'ve got it coming to them. *They*'ll get theirs and the world will be a better place with them not in it,' Truthful asserted.

'Yeh, *they* say we'd be better off without them.'

'How would *they* know?' Truthful replied, then did a double take. 'How come *they* are so powerful—if *they* don't know?'

'Perhaps *they* are born to it,' I suggested. 'With silver spoons in their mouths. Inherited money . . .'

'Or maybe *they* started work with the public service or the finance companies at an early age and were trained in bastardry,' Truthful replied, and thumped the bar with his fist. 'Anyway, *they* can all get well stuffed for mine!'

24

That the Melbourne–Sydney argument can be settled

HOW THE MELBOURNE–SYDNEY ARGUMENT WAS SETTLED

'Did you have a bet on the Melbourne Cup?' I asked Truthful Jones.

'That would be the last race I'd bet on,' Truthful replied. 'Too big a field and too many triers. Anyway, it would be better if the Melbourne Cup was never run. It causes too many arguments between Melbourne and Sydney people about horses and jockeys.'

'It's funny how Melbourne and Sydney people always argue, isn't it? Another Australian legend.'

'Well, I guess so, although they tell me the Russians argue over which is the best city, Moscow or Leningrad; and the Yanks over New York and Los Angeles.'

'Why do people go on like that?' I asked Truthful.

'In any country where the two biggest cities are just about equal size—or the capital city is a phoney like Canberra and Washington—nobody but nobody argues that those cities are better than anywhere—people argue about cities. But we settled the Melbourne–Sydney argument on neutral territory, one time. Did I ever tell you about it?'

'No. Have another drink and tell me.'

'Don't mind if I do. It happened in a pub, near the Victorian and New South Wales border—neutral territory. There were these two blokes: one from Melbourne, the other from Sydney. They were the best of mates, fought in the war together, worked together, drank together—but used to argue about Melbourne and Sydney.'

'Of course, these arguments are only a joke.'

'They start off as a joke, like between these two blokes I'm telling you about, Melbourne Mick and Sydney Sam. But they often get serious, I can tell you. They might start making sly little jokes about the harbour bridge being an oversized coathanger, or the Yarra being the only river in the world that flows upside down. Melbourne Mick would say: "The only city in the world where they have a public holiday for a horse race."

'And Sydney Sam would come back: "But more Sydney than Melbourne jockeys have ridden the Cup winner in the last ten years." So they'd switch to jockeys. Sydney Sam would talk about George Moore riding more winners every season than any Melbourne jockey. And Melbourne Mick would quote how Scobie Breasley won the English jockeys' premiership two years in a row. So they'd switch to horses and go at it hammer and tongs. Melbourne Mick would end up quoting Phar Lap's record; and Sydney Sam would refer to Tulloch's stake winnings. Well, I used to drink with them, see, and I was a neutral in the Melbourne–Sydney war. So I'd say: "Both Phar Lap and Tulloch are New Zealand-bred horses." '

'So that's how you settled the argument?' I asked.

'It wasn't that easy, mate. No, they come to blows more than once about football. Melbourne Mick would say: "Australian Rules draws bigger crowds in Melbourne than Rugby in Sydney." "What?" Sydney Sam would say, "that's not football, mate, it's aerial ping-pong." That aerial ping-pong crack was always good for a fight in the pub yard. After the fight, Melbourne Mick would start the argument again. "In Rugby they throw the ball all the time. A good Australian Rules player would kick a goal on a Rugby ground from the other end." Then I would intervene, see. "Hang on a minute, don't either of you realise that the only true game of football is soccer? They use the feet only, real football." '

'That should have settled that one?'

'Settled nothing. They'd get on to climate. Sydney Sam would make a sarcastic remark about it always raining in Melbourne; and Melbourne Mick would say he'd read in the paper that there were more sunny days a year in Melbourne than Sydney. They had three or four fights about the weather. So I wrote to that weather station in Queensland and got back a letter to say that Sydney actually had a higher rainfall than Melbourne but that Melbourne had less sunny days than Sydney.

'Then they'd change the subject to migration. I thought Melbourne Mick had Sydney Sam over the barrel. He proved on official figures that Melbourne attracted more migrants than Sydney. But old Sydney Sam said this was due to more migrants from London going to Melbourne. "And what's that got to do with it?" Melbourne Mick asked. "Well, the Thames is muddy, just like the Yarra." And out into the pub yard they went again.'

'Terrible thing to see two friends fighting like that, Truthful,' I said.

'It worried me, I can tell you. But I gradually broke them down on the Yarra and the bridge, horses and jockeys, football, climate and migration. And on the question of population I broke up a fight by explaining that, while Sydney had the bigger population, Melbourne was growing faster.'

'You should have been a diplomat.'

'It took more than a diplomat to stop them arguing about beer, mate. They had a fight every pay night about beer. This pub, being on the border, served both Melbourne and Sydney beer, in those days. Melbourne Mick drank Melbourne beer and Sydney Sam drank Sydney beer, needless to say. And they'd needle each other. "Melbourne beer has a higher alcoholic content," Mick would say. "That's why there's more alcoholics in Melbourne than Sydney," Sam would reply. "Sydney beer is thick and frothy like a milk shake," Melbourne Mick would argue. "Everybody knows Melbourne beer is the best. Some say it's because the water's more suitable." This would give Sam an opening. "I always knew Melbourne beer was watered." That was good for another fight.

'I tried everything to stop them. Even got the barman to serve Mick Sydney beer and Sam Melbourne beer—but they knew the difference. They each took one sip, spat it out and said: "What, are you trying to poison me?" They had so many fights over the real and imagined quality of Melbourne and Sydney beer, I was worried they would end up punchy. So one night I says to them: "Listen, mates, these arguments and fights over Melbourne and Sydney beer have got to stop. Tell you what I'll do. I'll send a sample of the best Melbourne and Sydney beer to the Commonwealth Scientific and Industrial Research Organisation for analysis. Will you abide by their decision?" Well, Mick and Sam were both of a scientific turn of mind, as you can see. So they agreed: if the CSIRO said both beers were excellent that would end the argument. "And," I says, "if they say one beer is better than the other, you have to accept the decision." They couldn't have agreed quicker.

'So I got a bottle of best Melbourne and Sydney beer, scraped the labels off, marked them A and B and sent them off with a letter to the CSIRO. Weeks went by and we got no reply. Melbourne Mick and Sydney Sam began to argue and sometimes fight over the likely result of the test.

'So I sent a telegram to the CSIRO. And back came the answer: "Thorough tests made stop regret inform you both horses have yellow jaundice." That's how we settled the argument between Melbourne and Sydney.'

25

That every battler could be a virtuoso—given the chance.

PIANISTS ARE BORN NOT MADE

'There's more untapped talent in this country than you can poke a stick at,' Truthful Jones said in the Carringbush Hotel. 'Trouble is, your average battler doesn't get a chance . . .'

I took up Truthful's theme. 'You're right, old mate. In Sydney there's more top-class actors unemployed per head of population than in any other city on earth . . . And in Melbourne, there's more good short-story writers who rarely get published than in any other city in the world.'

Truthful tilted his hat back. 'But what about those who never get a chance to be an unemployed actor or an unemployed musician or an unemployed writer?'

'You mean, Truthful, that the society is so set up that the average battler's children don't stand a chance to develop their talents?'

'That's nothing more than a simple fact!' Truthful exclaimed. 'It's a mystery to me how more than half the population seems to listen to daytime talkback bloody radio and to stations that run only rock or pop music. The media seem to run a line that if you listen to the ABC or like classical music, or want to be a composer or a dancer you're some kind of egghead or a poof!'

'The whole capitalist system is anti-poetic, anti-creative,' I agreed. 'It wants to make all the arts elitist from opera right across the board . . .'

'I saw an opera once,' Truthful said. '*La Bohème*, it was, and it was a bloody beauty! There were these four blokes, down to their last franc, and the landlord comes in to collect the rent; so they get him pissed and get him talkin' about young birds and then accuse him of bein' a dirty old man and throw him out. And the songs, you call 'em arias, don't you? The songs were bloody beautiful. "Your Tiny 'And is Frozen".'

Truthful shocked me and everyone else in the bar by singing a few lines of Puccini's aria: 'Your tiny 'and is frozen, let me warm it for you dear . . .'

I swallowed a laugh at the very sight and sound of Truthful singing Puccini and seriously developed his idea. 'I've been a member of various writers' groups over the years: the Realist

Writers, the Carringbush Writers ... And always these groups attract ordinary people with talent for writing, but most of them have a bash for a while and then give it up. I'll give you an example: the Melbourne *Age* runs a short-story competition every year about Christmas time. One year I did some of the reading of the manuscripts. There were 2,500 entries of which at least a thousand were good-class, publishable material—and they publish six. That happens every year. There must be thousands of good short stories lying in bottom drawers all over the country ...'

Truthful was so eager to continue that he bought a drink. 'You know, I used to be crook on rock music, but now I see that it's people's music. A few kids get hold of a guitar and a set of drums and they start makin' music, writin' their own songs. Did you know, there's 5,000 rock bands in Sydney alone. Fair dinkum, I read it in the paper ...'

'Then there's the folk scene,' I said. 'I spoke at a folk festival at Newcastle a few months ago and there was 400 people there. All of them could sing a bit, write a poem, dance. Just battlers from the Newcastle district and around the northern coalfields ...'

Truthful insisted, 'My point is not to mention the people who write short stories and songs and sing a bit of folk and rock but the people who never even think of doin' it because of the environment they're brought up in. Did I ever tell you about the time that Lightfingers Stratton pinched the Steinway grand piana orf a luxury liner many years ago when it was in Sydney docks for repairs?'

'No, I don't think you did—but I don't want to hear about it if it's another one of your bloody yarns about thieving on the waterfront ...'

'But those yarns of mine always make the point,' Truthful defended, 'that there's more thievin' done on the stock exchange than there is on the waterfront. But, as it turns out, Lightfingers Stratton wasn't a wharfie—he was just a common tealeaf, sold things that dropped off the back of trucks around the pubs, ran a few raffles and an SP book, but when the luxury liner came in to Sydney he read in the paper about all the expensive fittings and furniture on it ...'

'What the hell has this got to do with a battler not getting a chance to express his creative talent?' I asked impatiently.

'It's got a lot to do with it!' Truthful snapped. 'You've got a very bad habit of interrupting me in the middle of my stories. The old Lightfingers Stratton and his mate decided one day in a pub in George Street that they'd get a boat and go over to this luxury liner and steal the Steinway piana . . .'

'You're not gonna tell me that Lightfingers turned out to be a champion pianist just because he stole a Steinway piano?'

'A'course I'm not,' Truthful said. 'Lightfingers was tone deaf and so was his mate. But, anyway, over they go in the middle of the night, grabbed the grand goanna and lowered it down in a lifeboat, see. They get ashore, load the piana on a truck and hide it in the shed behind Lightfingers' house.'

'Be a hard thing to sell, a Steinway grand . . .'

'Wait till I tell yer. They go to a fence, see, a receiver of stolen goods named Octopus McGillicuddy. But the old Octopus wouldn't have a bar of it: "Do you know how many Steinway grands there are in the whole of Sydney? About a dozen. Want me to get arrested? That piana's as hot as the hobs of hell." Well, Lightfingers Jackson and his mate get their thinking caps on, and decide to telephone to professors of music and concert pianists. They started off asking for $5,000 but no takers. People were suspicious, like, you know how it is. So they drop the price to $2,000 and start peddling the piana around the clubs. Still no takers. And the police are out everywhere looking and the papers full of the mystery of the missing piana. Next they drop the price to 500 bucks and try the pubs. Ten o'clock closing had just come in and the publicans were bringing on a bit of a floor show—still no takers. And, boy, was this piana getting hot? A big reward was offered. Lightfingers and his mate were getting nervous . . .'

'But you said this story was called pianists are made not born. I don't see . . .'

'Barley Charley. My father always said, never get ahead of your story. At last, in desperation, they drop the price to 200 bucks and start ringing up the clubs in the bush. But nobody would touch that piano with a forty-foot pole. "Only thing to do," Lightfingers' mate said, "you'll have to learn to play it yourself."

' "Play it nothing," Lightfingers says. "I'm going to get rid of it." "How?" his mate asks. "Give it away, that's how, and quick, before we get nabbed with it." So they offer the Steinway grand to the local publican. "What's wrong with it?" he asks. "Must be something wrong with it, if you're giving it away." The same wherever they went; people wouldn't take it as a present. They ran around like a forger with a million dollar cheque. They rang up students and orphanages and convents—but nobody would take the piano.'

'I still can't see what this has to do with pianists being made not born.' I played straight man.

'Well, one night late, they sneak the Steinway grand piana out of the shed, on to the truck and away they go. They drive around for a while, then turn into a dead-end slum street and dump it there. Next morning, Lightfingers buys the papers but there's nothing about the piano. That afternoon, he buys the papers again. "We'll read all about it," he tells his mate. But there was not a word. And Lightfingers and his mate never saw or heard of the piano again from that day to this.'

'I suppose I should ask: I wonder whatever did become of that piano?'

'Well, I heard afterwards that there was an unemployed fella living in that street, had a large family, poor as a church mouse. One of his daughters, name of Anne, was a very promising pianist but this bloke couldn't afford to buy a piana for her to practise on. Imagine how he felt when he came out at dawn and saw there before his eyes—a Steinway grand piana. Well, he takes a look around, calls his missus and they drag it into the house.'

'The plot thickens.'

'That little kid practised six hours a day on that piano and she got so good that a professor from the Conservatorium gave her free lessons. I won't mention any names, but she's one of Australia's greatest pianists today. It's like I told you, pianists are made not born.'

26

That Australians value dogs more than people.

THE LEGEND OF THE TWO VALUABLE DOGS

Truthful Jones called from the door of the Carringbush Hotel bar. 'You look as worried as a bastard on Father's Day. What's the trouble?'

'Like Socrates, I'll answer a question with a question: what's the subject most popular with Australian yarn-spinners?'

'Sex?'

'Not even lukewarm.'

'Mothers-in-law?'

'No.'

'Doctors?'

'No.'

'AIDS?'

'No.'

'I'll play Socrates. Is it animal, vegetable or mineral?'

'Animal.'

'Horses, for sure . . . Don't tell me it's bloody crocodiles!'

'You're getting warm.'

Truthful became impatient. 'To be Frank and Hardy: I'd rather talk about the race time at Flemington.' He tilted his hat back. 'Horses! It's got to be horses . . .'

'It's dogs. Truthful, bloody dogs!'

'That figures,' Truthful said. 'Dogs played a vital role in the bush, and still do, for farmers, drovers and all. Me and Billy Borker had two valuable dogs one time, years ago. But don't get me talking about dogs or I might start telling lies. The most truthful man will tell lies about his dog. Even Billy Borker.'

'Sounds like a legend coming up. Have a drink and tell me about it,' I said.

'Me and old Billy Borker travelled together a bit in the old days, droving or prospecting, as yer know . . .'

'Here's your beer. Is that the same Billy Borker who claimed the big mosquitoes drove him out of the Territory?'

'One and the same. They actually carried him out. He went to sleep in an iron tank, and when the big mozzies stuck their stings through the walls of the tank, he bent them over with a hammer . . . And when he woke up he was on the banks of the Yarra in Melbourne, 2,000 miles away. A great man and a great yarn-spinner. He could tell this yarn better than I can but, him being slightly dead, my version will have to do.

'Me and Billy had been away droving, see, and we arrive in a one-pub town in Western Australia with a decent cheque to knock down. The pub was an old weatherboard building with the paint flaking off the outside, and there was some doubt if the inside had ever been painted. The publican's name was Big-hearted Paddy Murphy. There was no photographs in the bar and only one sign: "Do not ask for credit—a refusal might offend." Paddy was not a man to extend credit. But he was civil enough while you had money. Anyway, me and Billy Borker handed over our cheque to Paddy and said we'd cut it out. We sat in the bar all day and half the night talking about our dogs. I had a boxer-dingo cross (I've always been partial to that breed) and Billy had a bull-terrier-cattle-dog cross, a bitch. We took it in turns to tell stories about our dogs. Big-hearted Paddy and his missus listened politely. They even let us bed the dogs down on some bags in a corner of the bar and fed the dogs on the best cuts of meat. Treated the dogs like lords, as well as us—while our cheque lasted. The only row we had was when old Billy started pinching Florrie the barmaid on the bum and making rude suggestions to her. Murphy's missus took strong exception to this; threatened to kick us out. She was dead set against all manner of sin except alcoholic excess on the part of her husband's customers.

'Here's your beer. Thought this legend was to be about two dogs. You've hardly mentioned them so far . . .'

'Me and Billy mentioned them but . . . The first sign we got that our cheque was running out was when Big-hearted Paddy cast doubt on the veracity of one of Billy's dog stories. Billy reckoned that once when his herd of cattle was five short the dog counted them. "How could a dog count cattle?" asked Big-hearted Paddy. "He didn't count the cattle," Billy replied. "He counted the legs and divided by four." Big-hearted Paddy replied: "Well, if he's so smart tell him to start counting your beers. You've got money left for exactly five more each and not a drop more." Me and Billy managed to get ten more beers into us before Paddy called a halt. "A fair thing is a fair thing," Paddy said. "When I close at six, that's the finish." Billy did his block. "Get out, you Irish horse-thief! You've never closed this pub before midnight in thirty years." "Well, I'm closing tonight and I don't want to see you fellows here tomorrow."

'True to his word, Murphy turfed us out into the street at six o'clock, swags, dogs and all, and shut the pub. Me and old Billy sat on the doorstep with our dogs at our feet. "That there dog of mine was very savage as a pup," Billy said. "So bloody savage, I had to feed him with a long-handled shovel." And I said: "This here dog of mine rounded up a swarm of bees one time. He mustered them into a dog kennel, thinking it was a beehive."

' "Fancy that now," said Billy. "My dog is a great worker. With wild pigs, he'll grab a sow by the ear. A boar he'll grab by the tail to make it sit down. With young pigs he'll just hold them down with his paws, gentle as if they were babies. He'll grab a kangaroo by one arm, a bull or a buffalo by the nose. A great hunter, that there dog of mine. I was offered $500 for him by a local cocky the other day, but a'course I didn't take it."

'So I says: "Funny thing, not so long ago I was offered $500 for that there dog of mine, but I wouldn't take it, needless to say. Once I had a full sister to him. Used to work the two of them. One time I was bringing some cattle down from Queensland. There was a stampede and the herd broke, so I tells this here dog and his sister to round up the herd, which they did, but when I counted 'em there was five short, so I sent the dogs off to get them. The dogs didn't come back for a whole day so I went looking for them. Worth $500 each. I meets this drover, see, and I says: "Have you seen two boxer-dingos?" "Have I seen 'em!" he says. "They're amongst my herd." And so they were. The bitch had rounded up my five missing bulls and this here dog was on the back of one of them, scratching the hide looking for the brand.'

'Must have been great dogs, all right,' I admitted.

'Were they ever! Worth at least $500. But Billy was not going to be outdone when it came to dog stories. "One time," he said. "I went to Arabia with that there dog of mine to bring back a shipload of horses. Fifty miles off the Queensland coast a great storm blew up. The ship pitched and tossed. The horses took fright. And the captain said: 'Cut them horses loose and abandon ship.' Well, I cut the horses loose and they leapt into the raging sea. My dog, this here very dog, dived in after 'em. I got into the lifeboat and came ashore and there on the beach was all the horses. This here dog had rounded them up in the stormy sea and herded them ashore. Worth $500 if he's worth a cent." Billy Borker warmed to his subject: "That there dog of mine is as fast as a flying machine," he said. "She beat every dog in Bourke over 500 yards. Then a fella brought a greyhound racing dog up from Sydney and challenged this here dog of mine." '

'This story had better have a good ending, Truthful,' I said.

'It has one of those there echo endings that makes you listen after the story is finished.'

'Your trouble will be to keep me listening while the story is still going. Have another drink and get on with it.'

'Don't mind if I do. Where was I? Ah, yes, where the bloke with the greyhound challenges Billy Borker's dog. So Billy tells me, as serious as a judge: "Well, I tells this fella, 'My dog's due to have pups so I can't race her.' And the other fella tells him: 'That's only an excuse.' " So Billy did his block and agreed to let his bitch run a race.'

'Here's your beer. She couldn't beat a Sydney greyhound in her condition, surely,' I said doubtfully.

'Old Billy reckoned his bitch ran the race all right and the other dog never got a place . . .'

'Thought it was only a two-dog race.'

'It was, but Billy's dog had two pups at the turn into the straight and the pups ran second and third. He told me this without batting an eyelid. "And yer wonder why I won't take $500 for that bitch of mine!" he tells me, and just to keep me from throwing any doubts on his truthfulness—he used to get upset and go off his tucker if anyone cast aspersions on his truthfulness—he tells me: "And your dog is worth $500 as well and don't you ever forget it."

'Old Billy Borker rose to his feet, licked his lips and said: "Let's drink to our two valuable dogs." And I reminded him: "Big-hearted Paddy has cut our credit off." Old Billy goes berserk and starts kicking the pub door: "Come out, you black-hearted Irish scoundrel, and give two thirsty hard-working men a drink." Paddy's voice comes from inside the pub: "You'll get no more free drink here." With that he throws a sugar-bag of tucker out the window. "Here's a grub stake. Get on yer way, and good riddance to bad rubbish."

'Old Billy Borker turned to me and said: "What's the country coming to? Here we are with a thousand dollars' worth of dogs and can't get a drink in the town!" '

I laughed appreciatively. 'Great punchline. I like it.'

Truthful replied, 'And so you should. It's a legend for your book. That Australians value dogs more than people.'

That when you want work you can't find it and when you don't everyone offers you a job.

THE SUNDOWNER WHO PAID HIS FARE OUT OF WAGGA WAGGA

'Which was the worst depression—that of the eighties or that of the thirties?' I asked Truthful Jones in the Woolpack Inn, Parramatta.

'Six of one and half a dozen of the other,' Truthful replied. 'Many people in the eighties are in debt to hire-purchase companies, and when they become unemployed, they lose fridges, cars or even houses. Even those still employed are in hock to the plastic card purveyors at exorbitant interest. In the thirties, most people who lost jobs had no debts.'

'But remember,' I insisted, 'early in the thirties there was no dole at all: and later if a father was working, his sons couldn't get the dole—and *vice versa*. And if you collected rations or dole in one town, you had to move fifty miles before you could draw it the next week. The government contained the anger of the unemployed by keeping them moving. In the eighties depression they contain the unemployed by paying them just enough to eke out a miserable existence below the poverty line, with many young people homeless.'

'The unemployed don't move around so much now,' Truthful admitted. 'They get frustrated; and some turn to vandalism or drugs. And if they get heavily into drugs, they have to steal to feed their habit. Yeh, I'd come down on the side of this depression in the eighties being worst.' Truthful licked his lips. 'There's no such thing as a good depression—they call 'em recessions now, doesn't sound so bad. But Timetable Tommy, a famous bagman of the thirties, reckoned that the boom between depressions was bloody near as bad as the depressions themselves. I'm thirsty just thinking about it.'

Sensing a yarn, I bought two schooners of beer.

'Did I ever tell you about the sundowner who paid his fare out of Wagga Wagga?' Truthful Jones asked, sipping his beer.

'What's unusual about that?' I asked.

'What! Sundowners never paid fares. It was against the rules of the Bagmen's Union. You were on the track during the depression. You should have been a member of the Bagmen's Union. Would you believe that I wore herring tins for shoes once? And my wife, Clara—who always liked to put on side—wore condensed-milk tins for high heels?'

'This sundowner paid his fare during the thirties depression, did he?' I ventured.

'No, just after World War II, when the boom started. The way the system works is: a depression, a war, then a boom. They talk about dole bludgers who don't want to work, yet if a war started tomorrow there'd soon be no unemployment. I joined the army when the war broke out. Came straight off the track. The 6th Divvy was made up mainly of bagmen. First steady job we ever had was getting shot at. I joined up with Timetable Tommy. A very cultured man, he knew the time every train left every town in four states.

'Well, me and Timetable got discharged from the army in Queensland in 1946. Seeing as we hadn't paid a train fare since 1930, we jumped the rattler out of Brisbane by force of habit. We got to Albury easy enough, then decided to hitch-hike down the highway.

'We came on the old sundowner sitting under a peppercorn tree at Wodonga. And so help me—he's grilling a nice bit of

T-bone steak on a wire griller. Corks on his hat brim, a scraggy beard, about fourpence worth of old clothes on, eyes staring like holes burned in a blanket.

' "Where did you get the flash griller, mate?" I asked him.

' "Bought it at the ironmongers in Albury," he says.

' "That's a nice bit of steak," Timetable Tommy says.

' "I bought it at the butchers," the sundowner tells him.

'Tommy says: "Things *have* changed up on the track. Before the war, in the thirties, there were no jobs and you were lucky to get a handout of maggotty mutton."

'Anyway, the old fella gives us a bit of steak and we hop in. "The track's not what it was," he tells us, "people keep offering you work: there must be too much employment or not enough workers. You get handouts of cash sometimes. And I paid me fare on a train yesterday—first time in twenty years."

'The old sundowner told us he was up at Wagga Wagga asleep under a bridge when a farmer woke him up and said: "Do you want a job harvesting?"

' "Not me," he told him, "it's against me union principles."

' "Thirty pounds a week—and your keep," the farmer said, "double time for Saturdays and sleep in the house with sheets on the bed."

'The sundowner told me and Timetable Tommy that he had just decided to push off when up drove a Rolls-Royce and out got a flash cocky in leggings and riding breeches. "Sorry to disturb you, old son," he said. "Would you care for employment during the harvest? Fifty pounds a week, the use of my car at weekends. And you can sleep with my wife every Sunday night."

'The old sundowner was beginning to weaken. So he rolled his swag and legged it up the opposite bank and down to the railway station for the lick of his life. The passenger train was about to pull out. Too late to jump it. So the sundowner had to pay his fare.

'Me and Timetable asked him: "And where are you going now, old-timer?"

' "To the Strzelecki Ranges until after the harvest," he told us. "Nothing grows there except gum trees and bracken." '

'Does that story have a moral?' I asked Truthful.

'The moral is, mate,' Truthful answered, 'that there's either a famine or a feast—a boom or a depression. During a depression you can't find work; and during a boom just when you've got used to not working, every bastard you meet wants to offer you a job.'

That Darwinism was used to justify white racism.

ONE MAN'S DAMPER IS ANOTHER MAN'S SOUP

Truthful Jones said when I entered the bar of the Katherine Hotel: 'Been a bout of fisticuffs outside. A white fella and a black fella.'

'Who won?' I asked.

'The Abo. The white bloke picked him with racist talk and the black bloke flattened him. On for young and old, it was. Have a beer!'

'Thanks,' I said. 'Funny thing that: white Australians really believe Aborigines can't fight. That attitude began with white settlement . . .'

'Yeh,' Truthful said satirically. 'Real even fights in the early days: gunpowder against spears. The blackfella's ability to fight didn't begin with Dave Sands and Lionel Rose . . .'

'I'll drink to that. It began around Sydney Town 200 years ago . . . the Myall Creek massacre and so on . . .'

Truthful tilted his hat back. 'Been a lot of massacres since then, especially in the Northern Territory. The Conistoan Massacre and the Treacle Tinkler Massacre.'

'Never heard of the Treacle Tinkler Massacre. Where was Treacle Tinkler?'

'It was a man—not a place.'

'Why did they call him Treacle?'

'Well, he was one of those rough cattlemen in the old days—ate only damper and treacle—and expected everyone to do the same, including the Aboriginal tribe that lived and worked on his property.'

'That was donkey's years before the Aborigines were granted citizenship rights, a'course,' I said.

'No use granting citizenship rights unless they are paid enough money to exercise those rights,' Truthful Jones said. 'One of the Sydney Sunday papers had an article about it and they said that the Aborigines only spend their money on booze. Did you ever hear a boss ask a white man what he was going to spend his money on? Some mugs say that if they get equal pay the cattle stations will sack most of them. They've got to be joking. Easy to see they haven't been on a cattle station. Their Aborigines often live in humpies without water or furniture. And most of them are very skilled workers—musterers, horsemen, branders, and so on. The cattle stations couldn't do without them. Damper and salt beef is all they get to eat, but sometimes the pastoralists put some extra salt on the beef. And as the saying goes: one man's damper is another man's soup.'

'I thought the saying was: One man's meat is another man's poison,' I interrupted.

'Poison, that's the operative word,' Truthful said. 'In the early days of the Territory, when the white man came, he lived the same as the Aborigines. The Aborigines resented him taking their tribal lands and there was a lot of trouble including murder—yes, murder, mate—on both sides. But eventually the cattle men won and the Aboriginal tribes lived near the homesteads. They'd fed the white man at first on native tucker, yams, goanna, kangaroo, and so on. Then the white man brought the cattle in, and taught the Aborigines to work cattle. Later on, the Aborigines taught the white men as more came in; most of the station managers and jackeroos today were taught all they know by Aborigines.'

'Tell me about Treacle Tinkler,' I said. 'An illiterate, like most of the early cattlemen, I suppose.'

'No, he had a few books; one he kept beside his bed: *The*

Origin of the Species, by Charles Darwin. Well, he bought a few cattle and poddy-dodged a few more. Poddy-dodging means stealing unbranded cattle. In the old days there were a lot of unbranded cattle around. Old Treacle changed the natives' diet from damper and treacle to damper and beef—someone else's beef. "You don't need tea and sugar and treacle; that's white fella tucker," he used to tell them.'

'Well, after a few years he got a lot of cattle one way and another, and the natives learned to work them. And they worked long hours for no wages and lived on damper and stolen beef. But they began to get dissatisfied for some reason and kept asking old Treacle for tobaco, dresses for the lubras, sugar, sweets for the piccaninnies, and the rest. And cunning old Teacle used to say to them: "That hawker fella him bin coming soon. I bin write 'em down for you, bacca, dresses, sweets, jam, laughing-sided boots, shirts and all that white fella stuff." But every time the hawker came, old Treacle would say to the natives: "You bin seein' me write down all them white fella things for you, but that bloody hawker fella, him bin no good, him not give 'em me." And the old Treacle would start crying and continue through the tears: "I bin goin' away from here; that hawker him not treat me properly and you black fellas have been gettin' 'em nothing but beef and damper. He only give 'em me enough sugar and flour for meself, no dresses, no nothing. I bin going away from here and take 'em cattle with me" And the natives, who loved to work cattle, would cry with old Treacle, and the elder of the tribe would say: "No, boss, you stop 'em that cryin' now. You stay here and we work alla same as before." '

'Must have been a cunning bastard, Treacle.'

'Cunning as a lavatory rat. Cunning and force were the white man's weapons. But the natives got sick of watching him eating damper when they were run out, and drinking tea with sugar, so they started to knock off old Treacle's supplies. They had an ingenious way of pinching sugar; they used to get a straw of thick grass and poke it into the bottom of a bag and leak the sugar out. Sometimes old Treacle used to grab a bag of sugar and it would be empty except for a few pounds around the neck. But he was a philosophical old fella, in his own way, the old Treacle, so he used to say: "Ah, well, they're stealing half me sugar, but the bags have long necks and I'm still showing a profit." Yer see, Treacle was paid by the government to feed the natives, and he showed a profit, naturally. The cattle stations got a subsidy from Welfare to feed and clothe the natives and they got the natives' pensions and child endowment. There was more money in breeding Aborigines than breeding cattle, some of the station men said. Nigger farming, they called it.'

'You're making this up.'

'No way, but the natives got cheekier and they started to knock off Treacle's flour and baking powder. It got that way they were each eating more damper and sugar than Treacle himself, and gave up work. He got very upset about this, so he decided to teach them a lesson.'

'Here's your beer. Did he lecture them on honesty?'

'What? The kettle calling the pot black? Not on your life. He put strychnine into a bag of flour and baking powder. A'course, he put a big "POISON—NOT TO BE EATEN" sign on the bags. The natives couldn't read English. But it gave Treacle an alibi. His plan was to say that he intended using the flour and baking powder for poisoning dingoes.'

'Don't tell me the Aborigines ate the flour and baking powder?'

'They made the biggest damper in the history of the Territory and laid it on a granite rock. The tribe gathered around. First, the piccaninnies grabbed handfuls of the damper; soon they are grabbing their stomachs in agony and diving into the lagoon to put the fire out. All the time old Treacle is watching from behind a big rock, grinning to himself. Reckoned it was the greatest corroboree he ever saw. The men and the lubras then ate their share and held their stomachs in agony, then dived into the lagoon to put the fire out. They drank the water and forced mud down the kids' necks but pretty soon they were all dead—except one young lubra who wasn't hungry.'

'You don't honestly expect me to believe an outrageous story like that?' I said, then I felt impelled to add, 'But Treacle was a student of survival of the fittest: Darwin's theory could justify killing what he deemed to be an unfit, inferior people.'

'Ah, the old Treacle probably thought the book was about physical exercise; he didn't need to read books to be a racist. When the inside story of white Australia's treatment of Aborigines in the early days gets written, there's a lot of dreadful things going to come out, including the story of how Treacle poisoned the natives for stealing his gear.'

'Did he get arrested?'

'Naturally, but he got off on account of the "POISON" sign. Not his fault the natives couldn't read, he told the judge.'

'And what became of Treacle Tinkler?'

'Well, he married the lubra who lived because she didn't eat the damper.'

'Don't say they lived happily ever after!'

'Old Treacle lived happily for about twelve months, then he went into Darwin hospital with a high fever. The doctors couldn't find anything wrong with him but he was dead in a week. Natural causes, they put on the death certificate.'

'And was it?'

'Well, I don't rightly know, but they say the Aborigines have a poison they make by boiling green beetles. No test known to medical science can pick it. Anyway, they reckon this lubra used to do old Treacle's cooking and she made a brew of green beetle juice and slipped it into his soup. It's like I told yer, mate, one man's damper is another man's soup.'

I pondered the story with a feeling of shame.

'Don't get upset, mate, we'll be able to live with our past— when we accept that bastards like Treacle Smith pioneered this country.'

'And that Darwin's theory of the survival of the fittest was a bastard theory.'

Truthful tilted his hat back. 'You could be right: I always say it's not a theory so much as the way it's used. That applies to philosophy, religion and this newfangled fad about re-incarnation. Did I ever tell you the story about the actress who believed in reincarnation and came back as a politician?'

'No, I don't think you did. Tell me about her.'

'Have to be going: got to catch the shop to buy a tin of treacle . . .'

29

That the hunger for knowledge is more powerful than advertising.

THE HUNGER FOR KNOWLEDGE

'What's the book, Truthful?' I asked, as I walked into the bar of the New Brighton Hotel, in Manly.

'*A Modern Prospector's Guide*. How to find gold in ten easy lessons.'

'Do you read much?' I asked.

'A fair bit. Not as much as I did before television was invented, but . . .'

'Books are a wonderful thing,' said I, and ordered two beers.

'Must be a funny game, writing. A writer writes a book—on his own. And a reader reads it—on his own. No audience like a musician or an actor—or a yarn-spinner,' said Truthful thoughtfully.

'Think of the knowledge spread by books through the ages,' I replied.

'Yes, I've learned a lot from books—but I don't go for those made-up stories about murderers, thieves, businessmen . . .'

'Are you thinking of going prospecting, Truthful?'

'I've done a lot of prospecting in me time. Like to keep up

to date. Matter of fact, I was out prospecting when I learned the real power of the hunger for knowledge. Me and Time-table Tommy went prospecting north of Kalgoorlie. In the desert, a hundred miles from the nearest railhead. Well, we worked like slaves to sink a deep shaft. Thought we were on a quartz reef, but struck solid rock. Timetable got jack of it, after that, so when the truck came out with mail and the weekly supplies of grub and water, he took a lift back and left me there. Well, I kept digging. Slow work on your own; and very lonely, especially at night. Used to lie awake listening to the dingos howling. Then, one night, I saw a light in the distance. Seemed to be fairly close by, so I headed towards it. I must have walked three or four miles: a single light always seems closer than it really is in the bush at night. There was a crescent moon casting weird shadows . . .'

'I don't see what this has to do with the hunger for knowledge.'

'Wait till I tell you. Anyway, eventually I get near this light; a carbide lamp in a lean-to.'

'Lean-to?'

'A poor man's tent. Like an Aboriginal's mia mia. This one was made of logs and bark. I see an old codger sitting on a small box beside a big box with the lamp on it. He's shuffling a pack of cards. So I thinks, "A poker school." The mateship of a game of cards was just what I needed. I'm just going to speak, when the old fella deals himself about twelve cards. He fans them out in his hand, looks at them, then turns them face down on the box. Then he screws up his face and reels off the cards in a high-pitched cackling voice. "Ten of hearts, jack of diamonds, seven of clubs, ace of spades, six of hearts . . ." I go a bit closer and you should have seen him. Eyes sticking out like you could knock them off with a stick. Long white hair, and a moustache and beard. Bony hands like skeleton's covered with withered yellow leather. Bare, dirty feet. Holes in the knees of his old dungarees and a flannel singlet gone hard with sweat and dust. He deals himself another hand, turns the cards down on the table. And he reels off the cards again. "Ace of clubs, four of hearts, seven of diamonds, jack of

139

spades, ten of clubs . . ." I thinks, "What have I struck here?" He's there on his Pat Malone, see, talking to himself, silly as a two bob watch.'

'What was he doing?' I asked.

'That's what I was wondering. He's got an old clock there. So he winds it up and puts it on the box. Then he steps back to the entrance and listens with his hand cupped around his ear. And he backs away from the clock towards me, with his hand to his ear, listening. Before I could get away, he bumps into me, see, and swings around. One of those mad hermits who hang around old goldfields until they die. He put the wind up me, I can tell yer.'

'I'll bet he did. Get on with the story,' I urged.

' "What's your name?" he asks me, as if it was natural for someone to stumble into his camp in the middle of the night. "Truthful Jones," I says, backing away. He repeats the name: "Truthful Jones," then dashes into the hut, grabs the lamp, and holds it in front of my face. "Truthful Jones," he says. "Eyes blue. Complexion dark. Height five foot eleven. I'll remember you if we meet again."

'What was the purpose of his repeating the denomination of the cards, listening to the clock, and committing your name and description to memory?' I asked, intrigued.

'Well, it turned out that he'd seen an advertisement in an old newspaper that had come out to his camp wrapped around some groceries. He cut out the coupon and took one of them courses in Pelmanism that used to be advertised. You know: "Train the mind, memory, and personality. Strengthen your will. Improve your memory and hearing. Increase your powers of concentration, become a business executive." I couldn't help thinking: what use would such a course be to him? There he was, a hundred miles from the railway, 150 miles from the nearest human habitation, seventy-five years old, and as mad as a hatter. What would he want with a course in Pelmanism?'

'Yes, it shows the power of the hunger for knowledge, all right,' I nodded.

'Either that or the power of advertising. I've never been able to decide which,' he said as he tilted his hat back and scratched his chin.

30

That Australians always want to be somewhere else.

NOT LIKE HERE IN WOOLLOOMOOLOO

Truthful Jones turned up at the Carringbush Hotel to discuss Australian legends. 'We're running out of ideas,' he said.

'That Australian taxi drivers are thieves,' I ventured.

'No,' Truthful said. 'They weren't born thieves; it's what you call an occupational disease. What about our attitude to foreign places, the "anywhere but here" syndrome?'

'You mean the idea that Australians have to succeed overseas before they can succeed in Australia, the overseas-made syndrome, the fight in foreign wars syndrome?'

'Something like that,' Truthful replied, tilting his hat back. 'For example, did I ever tell you about the fella from Woolloomooloo whose life's ambition was to go to Paris?'

'No, I don't think you did. Have a drink and tell me about him.'

'Thanks. Well, this fella used to be always saying he'd like to go to Paris, see. Said it in the pub. Said it nearly every day at smoko. Wharfie, he was. Couldn't afford a trip on the Manly ferry—but wanted to go to Paris.'

'Oh, I don't know—here's your beer—wharfies don't make bad money.'

'Three hundred dollars a week and half the cargo, some mugs reckon. Don't you believe it. There's no more thieving goes on there than on the stock exchange, I can tell you. Anyway, this bloke kept saying he wanted to go to Paris. Used to stand in the pub at Woolloomooloo with his mates of a Saturday morning, spending his last dollar on beer and saying he wanted to go to Paris. Funny thing that, isn't it? People always want to be somewhere else, to do things they can't do . . .'

'I think I've heard you say that before. Did this fella get to Paris?'

'There you go again. Trying to make me get ahead of my story. As I was saying before you so rudely interrupted, people are always wanting to be someone else. I've heard Bob Hawke wanted to be a whisky-taster at the Royal Show; that's why he gave up the booze. A bloke told me that in a pub in Kalgoorlie . . . Anyway, this fella from Woolloomooloo kept saying he'd like to go to Paris. Even said it to his wife in bed one night. She took a jaded view of his ambition, as you can understand, a woman will trust a man anywhere except in Paris—that didn't stop him wanting to go. As it turned out, his wife died after ptomaine poisoning from drinking you-know-who's beer. And being a widower increased his ambition to go to Paris . . .'

'Aw, come on! Did he go or not?'

'Coming to that. It turned out that one Saturday morning his mates were standing in the pub at Woolloomooloo when he rushed in and said he'd won the lottery. Shouted for the bar to prove it. Well, needless to say, his mates gave him plenty of advice. You can always get advice on how to spend money but never how to earn it . . .'

'Did he go to Paris or not? Here, have another drink.'

'Just to be sociable. One bloke suggested he should send his kids to university. "What," he answered, "and turn them into toffs and scabs? Not on your bloody life." "Buy yourself a house," another fella urged. "The old house I'm living in has done me for twenty years," he told him. "Well, buy a big Yankee car," someone else advised. "Can't drive a car," he said. "Well, buy a pushbike," another of his mates suggested. "Haven't got a peddler's licence," he replied. "It's no good arguing with me. I'm going to Paris. And I'm not coming back until all the money's gone." Within a week, he jobbed the panno, snatched his time and bought an air ticket to gay Paree.'

'Here's your beer. How did he get on?'

'Thanks. Matter of fact nothing more was heard from him . . .'

'Well, that's a poor sort of a story, that is. No point to it. There's no myth in that yarn.'

'Give me time; give me time. What goes up must come down. His mates often wondered what became of him. I was about to say that he was never heard of again—until one Saturday his mates arrived at the pub as usual, and there he was, large as life, standing in the corner all dressed up to go on afternoon shift, spending his last dollar on beer.'

'Spent the lot, had he?'

'A'course he had. No good ever came of a working man winning the lottery. Well, his mates crowded around him. And asked a lot of questions—about Paris, needless to say. They asked more questions than Johnny Carson. "What was the weather like in Paris?" "Not like here in Woolloomooloo. It was beautiful. I was there for six months in the spring and summer and the sun shining every day. Not too hot, not too cold. Not like here in Woolloomooloo where it's either too hot or too cold, either raining cats and dogs or a drought. Not like here in Woolloomooloo, I can tell you." "And what was the tucker like in Paris?" another fellow queried. "The tucker was beautiful," he told them. "Not like here in Woolloomooloo. You sit on the footpath and have your meals and watch the crowds go by while you sip your coffee. And the food? Delicious! Not cooked too much; not too underdone. Turtle soup, steak, and beautiful cheese—not like the bunghole here in Woolloomooloo—and frogs' legs done in beautiful sauce. They use seasoning in the sauce that would make the sole of a leper's boot taste like a *filet mignon*. Boy, that was tucker. Not like the pies and sausages you get at the hamburger joints and

Greek cafés here in Woolloomooloo. And glorious wine, the nectar of the gods! And German beer! Not like the watered-down grog you get here in Woolloomooloo. . ." '

'You make me feel thirsty. Have another beer.'

'Don't mind if I do. Mightn't be as good as in Paris, but I'll force it down. Well, they kept asking him about Paris. "Did you go to one of them there night clubs, where the women dance in the nude?" another mate asked. "I went to the Folies Bergère every night." "And what was it like?" "Not like these crummy floor shows here in Woolloomooloo, I can tell you. It was terrific. Music. Champagne. Floor show. Dancing girls, with nothing on, not a stitch. Not like here in Woolloo-mooloo." '

'I still can't see any point in this story . . .,' I said, worried we'd never get enough legends together for this book.

'Give me time to finish. Another bloke says to him: "And what were those French women like?" "Ah, not like these bags here in Woolloomooloo who are either too fat or too thin, too tall or too short. And mutton done up as lamb, most of them. These French women are glorious—not too fat, not too thin, not too tall, not too short. Beautiful clothes and perfect figures. An old French bag is better looking than a teenage model here in Woolloomooloo." '

'Here's your beer. He was real wrapped up in Paris, all right.'

'You can say that again. And they asked him plenty of questions—like a bosses' lawyer in the Arbitration Court. "They'd treat you well, those French women, I s'pose," another fella said. "Would they ever. Champagne and a chicken dinner chucked in." He got his money's worth in Paris, by the sound of him—"not like here in Woolloomooloo".'

'There's no end to this story by the sound of it.'

'All good things come to an end—like this bloke's trip to Paris. At last one fella asked him: "Did you ever screw a French woman?" "My bloody oath, I did," he replied. "And what was it like?" Well, that rocked him a bit. He looked this way and that, drained his last beer and said: "Oh, just like here in Woolloomooloo, come to think of it. Just like here in Woolloomooloo." '

'Yes, not bad. Real good, as a matter of fact. It grows on you, that story. Have another drink on the strength of it.'

'Not now,' Truthful grinned. 'I've just got time to catch the lottery office before it closes. Think I'll buy a few tickets. Wouldn't mind a trip to Paris meself.'

31

That you can't win on the racetrack—even when you pick the card.

THE WORLD'S WORST URGER

There we were in the Woolpack Inn, Parramatta, discussing horseracing.

'Did you back a winner Saturday, Truthful?' I asked.

'No, I couldn't back a winner in a two-horse race if one of them had three legs,' replied Truthful.

'You used to get some good tips,' I remarked.

'Listening to tips brought me undone. There's too many urgers around,' he replied.

'Urgers? What's an urger?'

'An urger is a bloke who slings out tips and asks for a cut if one of them wins. Did I ever tell you about the world's worst urger?'

'No. You've told me about the world's worst worrier and the world's worst whinger. Have another drink and tell me about the world's worst urger.'

'Don't mind if I do. Not a bad drop of beer, this. He operates in Sydney. They call him "Don't Tell a Soul—the world's worst urger". But the story is not really about him at all. It's about two mad punters, the Parrot and Hot Horse Herbie.'

'You get some rare nicknames in your stories,' I commented.

'Every nickname has a meaning behind it. The Parrot repeats everything you tell him. And Hot Horse Herbie loves the punt. Only works to get a bank to gamble on horses. Goes to every race meeting held in Sydney. They called off a meeting at Rosehill the other week because old Hot Horse Herbie was sick and couldn't go.'

'Must have been a keen punter, all right. Here's your beer.'

'Was he ever? Only book he'd ever read was the race book. A good judge of form, but usually lost on account of he always took off his head and put on a pumpkin when he went to the races,' Truthful replied.

'The Parrot was a sucker for a tip, see, always listening to tips and repeating them. Hot Horse Herbie used to nag him about it. "You're a shrewd student of form, weights, distances, betting habits of trainers, state of the track, horses for courses and the betting market. Why listen to tips?" But the

Parrot couldn't help himself. All great men have a fatal weakness.

'Well, the Parrot and Hot Horse Herbie meet at the pub one Saturday morning and the Parrot says: "Hot Horse, old mate, you're looking at the man who's going to back the card at Randwick today. I've studied all the form guides, picked one horse in every race and they're all going to win. I can feel it in me water." Hot Horse replied: "Trouble is, you'll listen to tips. You're a natural-born victim for urgers." The Parrot gets a bit niggly and he tells Hot Horse: "Your tips have cost me more money than I could poke a stick at."

'Anyway, this particular day, the Parrot swears he won't listen to tips. "Won't even listen to your tips," he tells Hot Horse Herbie. "I'll stay on me own all day. We'll separate and meet after the last race. I'll back the card for the first time in history. Here's the list of horses I'm going to back." '

'This story better have a good ending.'

'Well, off they choof to Royal Randwick. They arrange a meeting place and the Parrot dashes in to the betting ring. It was that one day in a lifetime that comes to every punter when he just knows he's going to back winners. The Parrot pulls out a twenty-dollar bill and is just going to hand it to a bookie when a man comes out of the crowd, soft and slow, like a rat out of a drain pipe. He grabs the Parrot's arm. A little bloke with a ginger moustache, wearing a spotted bow-tie, pointy-toed tan shoes and a narrow-brimmed hat with a yellow feather in the band. "Just a moment," he says to the Parrot. "I know you're a keen well-informed student of the turf, a veteran of the long war against the bookmakers, but on this occasion you are making a slight error, to wit, you're backing the wrong horse. Don't tell a soul, but the second favourite at the attractive odds of four-to-one is over the line. I ought to know; the trainer's wife is my wife's second cousin by marriage . . .'

'The plot thickens,' I said.

'Well, the Parrot switches and backs the second favourite. The horse he had intended to back romped in and the horse the urger tipped him ran unplaced. "If ever I get hold of the little fella with the ginger moustache, I'll wring his neck," he muttered as he came down from the grandstand. "I won't listen to anyone else; and I'll still back six winners out of seven races."

'Up he trots to the rails bookies. "My fancy will win this for sure, third favourite at five-to-one. Ron Quinton is riding the favourite but it couldn't win; only favourite because he's riding it; he can't come home without a horse." The Parrot takes out a ten-dollar note. "Ten dollars on . . ." '

'Don't tell me the little bloke with the ginger moustache came back after putting him off a winner.'

'Ah, urgers have more front than Myer's. He says to the Parrot: "Shake hands with the man that's just shaken hands with Mick Dittman." The Parrot shakes hands and he's ready to abuse old Don't Tell a Soul but he can't get a word in edgeways. "Don't tell a soul, but I've just been in the jockeys' room talking to Mick and he says the favourite can't get beat. He rode it a secret gallop on Thursday. Don't tell a soul." '

'And the Parrot listened to him?'

'A sucker for a tip, like I told yer—and you must admit it would be hard to resist. So the Parrot switches again.'

'And the horse he was going to back won again?'

'Only just. The Parrot tears up his betting brief like a parson ripping a lottery ticket. Mad as a meat axe. "Just let me get my hands on the little monster with the ginger moustache . . ."

'Just as Parrot is about to make his bet on the next race Don't Tell a Soul sidles up to him. "Admittedly, my friend," he says, "I've done you a bad turn, but I meant well. I'd like to make it up to you in some small way. Wait right here and I'll go over to the stalls, and see a trainer friend of mine who's got one in this race. If they declare for it, it will win by panels of fences. Don't go away."

'Well, the old Parrot had intended to wring his neck, but old Don't Tell a Soul could sell a tip to an anti-gambling crusader in ten seconds flat. Eventually, the urger comes back and says: "Don't tell a soul: number six, Hairy Legs, is home and hosed. You'll get a long price; it's an SP job; they're backing it in Hobart and Darwin. Don't tell a soul."

'Meanwhile Hot Horse is over the bar telling their friends how the Parrot has backed the first three winners and has declared himself a moral to back the card. Anyway, Don't Tell a Soul tells the Parrot that the odds-on favourite is the only trier in the next race. This was after he had ducked under a powerful left hook the Parrot threw at him. Don't Tell a Soul talked him out of backing the winners of the fifth and sixth races. A'course, he was trying hard to tip the Parrot winners, then touch him for some of his winnings; he was just a bit unlucky, that's all.

'Anyway, comes the last race, the Parrot had picked the winner of six races in a row and had not backed them. Down to his last ten dollars. Just going to hand the bookmaker the note when up sidles Don't Tell a Soul and says: "You've had a bit of bad luck here today and I feel in some small measure responsible for the worn tread in your currency, so I have toiled and connived to find a means of restoring your solvency. In short, I have obtained, at great expense, inside information about a thirty-to-one pop in the last race." The Parrot had had enough. "You couldn't pick a winner if you had the Sunday papers on Saturday morning. I'd have backed six in a row if I hadn't listened to you. I'm backing my own fancy, the favourite."

'The urger was cunning. "Not much use backing a two-to-one winner at this stage. You're further behind than Walla Walla. Long shot your only hope; get back your losses with interest. And I'm telling you, my friend, Sun God will win the last at thirty-three-to-one. Don't tell a soul and don't come moaning to me if it wins and you don't back it."

'The Parrot had to admit the urger's argument was sound; it was his only hope. So he backs Sun God and goes up into the stand to watch the race. The field turns for home with Sun God leading by four lengths. The Parrot was just reaching for his ticket, 330 lovely dollars to ten, when out of the ruck comes the favourite. A length, half a length, the favourite gaining on Sun God—a neck, then head and head to the post. The Parrot is yelling and listening to the broadcaster over the amplifiers at the same time. "Photo finish. But I'll bet London to a brick on, the favourite has won; Sun God second."

'Parrot tears up his ticket and goes to meet Hot Horse

Herbie. "Good luck to you, Parrot, you've backed the card; your lifelong ambition." The Parrot hangs his head and manages to mutter: "I never had a collect all day, never backed one winner." "What! Don't tell me you've been listening to tips again." "Every time I went to have a bet this little bloke came up to me . . ." Hot Horse Herbie sniffs the air. "Not a little bloke with a ginger moustache, spotted bow-tie, pointy-toed shoes and narrow-brimmed hat, by any chance?" "Him and none other," admits the Parrot. "Ah," says Hot Horse, disgusted, "that's Don't Tell a Soul, the world's worst urger. No use cryin' over spilt milk, mate. That'll teach you to listen to tips. Go and get a couple of nice hot pies and then we'll go down to the pub." He dips into his kick and gives Parrot the money. "Here, get two lovely hot pies with sauce. You know how I love pies."

'Away runs Parrot and comes back with two saveloys and mustard. "What's this?" yells Hot Horse Herbie. "I don't like saveloys, I told you to get pies." The Parrot replies: "Well, it was this way. I ordered two pies with sauce, when up came the little bloke with the ginger moustache . . ." '

'Now I've heard everything,' I said, grinning.

'No, you haven't,' replied Truthful. 'Did I ever tell you about the time the world's worst urger met Frank Duval?'

'No. Have another drink and tell me about it.'

'Don't mind if I do. Well, Frank Duval and the world's worst urger were at the races in Wagga Wagga. As I said, this fella could talk a nun into becoming a prostitute without raising his voice. But he couldn't talk those Wagga cockies into buying his tip. He kept telling them: "Don't tell a soul, but Gloves Off will win the Wagga Cup by panels of fencing. The trainer's sister is my mother-in-law's cousin." But the Wagga cockies were a bit suspicious, like. Then he sees Frank Duval going into the didee, see, so he follows him in.'

'Did Don't Tell a Soul ask Frank Duval for a tip?'

'Not on your life he didn't. He follows Frank Duval into the didee and he says. "Mr Duval, you're a millionaire. You own tin mines in the Northern Territory, a dozen racehorses and half of Hong Kong. And you've got your own private aeroplane. Well, I'm only a battler, Mr Duval. If roast turkey was a penny a ton, I wouldn't be able to afford a feather out of a vulture's tail. But I've got a tip for the Cup, see." And Frank Duval says. "I don't need your tips. My own horse is favourite." The world's worst urger says: "I'm not trying to sell you a tip. I'm trying to sell a tip to those local farmers out there. And I want you to do me a favour. When you come out of here you'll see me talking to them, see, and you come over and say: 'Ah, there, Ernie, old mate (my name's Ernie), how are you going? I've got a winner for you.' That's all you have to do. Won't cost you anything. You used to be a battler yourself once." '

'Don't tell me Frank Duval lent his name to a thing like that.'

'That's what he said to his friends when he came out of the didee. He told them what the world's worst urger wanted him to do. "I can't lend my name to a thing like that," he said to them. One of Frank Duval's friends says to him: "Ah, go on Frank, it won't cost you anything." And being a bit of a hard case urged him on: "He's only a battler, Frank, give him a go. Just for the fun of it." So Frank Duval finally goes over to Don't Tell a Soul and he says: "Ah, there, Ernie, how are you? I've got a winner for you."

'He replied: "Ah, piss off, Frank, can't you see I'm busy? I've got a winner of me own." '

'He wasn't satisfied to get Frank Duval to help, he had to rubbish him as well,' I said.

'That's not the point. The cockies were very impressed: the world's worst urger didn't need Frank Duval's tip, he had a better one of his own.'

'I like that one.'

'Yes, yer see, the most important news never gets into the papers.'

32

That workers' compensation is a God-given right.

THE GREATEST COMPO DOCTOR IN THE SOUTHERN HEMISPHERE

'You don't look too good today, Truthful.'

'Sick as a swagman's dog. On compo.'

'What's the trouble?'

'Crook back,' Truthful answered.

'That's an old workers' compensation trick. Have a drink.'

'I'll force one down just to be sociable,' Truthful said. 'Just think about it: what hope would a worker have without a bit of honest compo?'

'No hope, I guess—but I see the so-called Labor Government is going to cut back on workers' compensation . . .'

'What's the world comin' to?' Truthful said. 'Workers' compensation is a God-given right.'

'Y'know, Truthful,' I said, pushing his beer under his nose, 'I've got a theory about the prevalence of compo claims in this country—and of faked car accident claims . . . The statistics show, for instance that 15 per cent of car accident claims are faked.'

'So!' Truthful said, gulping his beer.

'Well, y'see, Australians will trick the bosses, talk about them behind their backs, but not confront them. Comes from our convict beginnings. Fiddle around the rules but avoid getting a flogging. During the boom years of the fifties and sixties, the unions used their power to gain shorter hours, better conditions, pay for unworked overtime ... so-called work practices. And now the boom is over the bosses are taking it all back.'

'So!' Truthful repeated.

I felt out of place, like a man farting in a cathedral, telling Truthful this theory, but now it was out I had to defend it. 'What I mean is, while the workers had the upper hand they should have fought for fundamental changes, for a better social system. There's gotta be a reason why our working-class folklore is full of stories about thieving, bludging and workers' compo perks. Take that seaman we knew called Fingers: he'd chopped orf three fingers on each hand to get compo, knew how much they paid on each knuckle ...'

'An extreme case,' Truthful replied. 'And it's no reason to go around callin' me a liar. It so happens that my back *is* crook but the doctor didn't believe me, either. "Bend down and pick up that piece of paper," he says. I bent down and couldn't get up again. And he says: "You're the greatest actor since John Barrymore." It's always the same; when you're telling the truth no-one believes you—especially compo doctors. Compensation doctors are supposed to obey the ethics of the profession, but I've struck a few that could have fooled me. A compo doctor's job is to save the insurance companies money by passing you fit for work. In the old days, a compo doctor would send a blind man back to work driving a truck. One actually did ...'

'I don't believe it.'

'Positive fact. I knew a compo doctor who sent a miner back to work with a broken neck after an explosion in the Kurri Kurri mine. After that, sick miners used to walk fifty miles to Newcastle to avoid him.'

'Have you ever met a good compensation doctor?' I asked Truthful, entering into his theme.

'Well, come to think of it, I have. When I was at sea I struck the greatest compo doctor in the Southern Hemisphere. A shipping company's doctor, he was. Name of Hawkins, at

Newcastle. He gave me a fortnight one time for a sore throat I got singing "The Wild Colonial Boy" at a union social.'

'You don't tell.'

'Positive fact. His dead-set minimum was a fortnight, whether there was anything wrong with you or not.'

'How did he get that way?'

'Well, there was various theories. Some said he had once sent a seaman back to work with a bad appendix which burst off Nobby's Head lighthouse and he died. Anyway, after that Doctor Hawkins put 'em all on compo—regardless.'

'Must have been popular with the company,' I laughed.

'You can say that again. As popular as a poker machine at a parsons' picnic. Was popular with steel workers, seamen and wharfies but . . . Yeh, he gave out compo without fear or favour. It used to be funny at the clinic. Six doctors there. All the compo cases outside Doctor Hawkins' door. Expectant women and old pensioners with colds or malnutrition went to the other doctors; but all the compo cases waited in a long queue for Doctor Hawkins. No more sick workers being sent back to work. No more workers playing compo tricks: no-one in Newcastle bothered using the old scrubbing brush to create rashes or clamping a tobacco tin over the skin to get a nice neat compo cut. Doctor Hawkins should have been knighted, a lot of people reckoned. The most popular man in the district. Yet some people were crook on him—especially captains of coastal ships sailing out of Newcastle.'

'Why was that?'

'Well, every time a ship came into Newcastle, some of the crew would pay off on compo. Then the second mate and the engineer would have to hang around the seamen's pick-up every day waiting for a full crew. There was one skipper on the old freighter *Iron River*; Mad Mick Burton, they called him. Swore he'd get rid of Doctor Hawkins if it was the last thing he did. Mad Mick had never been sick in his life and reckoned everyone else should be the same. "I'll get rid of that Hawkins some day and save the company a fortune," he used to tell the second mate.

'Anyway, to cut a long story short, the old *Iron River* sailed into Newcastle just before Christmas—and half the crew made a call on Doctor Hawkins and paid off on compo. Mad Mick Burton hit the roof. The mate and the engineer went to the pick-up every day but there was no labour available on account of the festive season. Mad Mick had had enough. He called a meeting of the officers midships and he says: "I'm going to put a stop to this Hawkins once and for all. I'm going up to the clinic to see him. I'll tell him a thing or two." '

'And how did he get on?'

'Well, Mad Mick choofs off up to the clinic to see Doctor Hawkins. The officers wait for him. The first mate says: "Captain Burton will put a stop to this crazy compo and get the ships turning around again." The chief engineer says: "I hope he doesn't do anything violent." Hours go by and they wait at the top of the gangway. At last they see Mad Mick coming along the wharf. As he comes up the gangway, the first mate says: "Well, skipper, did you see Doctor Hawkins?" "I saw him all right," the skipper says. "Did you tell him off?" "I'm a sick man," the captain replies. "A chill on the kidneys. Doctor Hawkins paid me off on a month's compo." '

'And what became of Doctor Hawkins?'

'He died eventually. Had the biggest funeral ever held in Newcastle. The greatest compo doctor in the Southern Hemisphere.'

'I still think we'd 'a been better off fighting for socialism, workers' control, than for compo and super . . .' I mused.

Truthful scratched his head—and actually bought a drink.

33

That you should never take advice from a barber.

WHAT DO YOU RECKON?

'I see you've had a haircut, Truthful,' I said and sipped my beer.

'Yeh, a haircut and a lot of advice. Funny thing how barbers always give advice. This bloke never stopped talking all the time I was in the shop.'

'Did he give you good advice?' I asked.

'Not him. My father always said: "Never back odds-on favourites, run upstairs, or take advice from a barber." Funny thing, I knew a bloke one time who wouldn't turn around without seeking the advice of the local barber. Bloke by the name of What Do You Reckon Johnson. Lived in Footscray. His favourite saying was "What do you reckon?", especially when he was in the barber's shop. His barber, Bush Lawyer Bloggs, was a frustrated lawyer who would advise anybody on any subject under the sun, especially his mate, What Do You Reckon. He advised him on horseracing, women, the weather, fish bait, altercations with the gendarmes, income tax, medical treatment, politics and dandruff.'

'He was well named—bush lawyer. He was the genuine article.'

'Was he ever! The greatest bloody knowall this side of the black stump. Would be flat out writing his name, but thought he knew everything. He could talk an alcoholic out of a wine shop without speaking above a whisper. One time he advised his mate on a slight case of larceny (old What Do You Reckon was a bit of a tealeaf in a small way). He'd knocked off some cigarettes. As soon as he gets out on bail, he consults Bush Lawyer Bloggs. "What do you reckon?" he asks. After studying the brief briefly, the bush lawyer replied: "A simple case—as soon as the beak enters, you get up and say: 'I want to make a legal submission'." So What Do You Reckon goes to court. Before the magistrate could sit down, he leaps to his feet and says: "I want to make a legal submission." The beak glares at him: "What kind of legal submission would you be wanting to make?" Old What Do you Reckon repeats what the bush lawyer told him to say: "I do not wish to proceed with this case," he tells the beak.'

'Well, naturally. Don't tell me he got off.'

'Got an extra month in jail for contempt of court, as a matter of fact. While he was in jail, Bush Lawyer Bloggs came to visit him. "What happened?" he asked. What Do You Reckon told him. "They can't do that," the bush lawyer said shrewdly. "They can't do that."'

'You better have another beer and get on with your story. By the way, what's the origin of the term "bush lawyer"?'

'Well, in the old days in the bush, there were no registered lawyers, so some half-shrewd mug, usually a barber, would set himself up to advise all and sundry. So now anyone who throws around a lot of free advice is called a bush lawyer.'

'I suppose What Do You Reckon Johnson lost faith in Bush Lawyer Bloggs after that experience.'

'Dropped him like a hot spud. Even changed his barber so he wouldn't have to listen to any more advice. People have great faith in barristers and solicitors, for some reason—and they're only bush lawyers with a university degree. Anyway, What Do You Reckon Johnson gave away listening to advice from barbers and started buying lottery tickets instead. Eventually he won first prize.'

'Here's your beer. What did he do with the money?'

'Decided to go for an air trip to Europe. When the bush
lawyer heard about it, he was very upset. Called around to
What Do You Reckon's house on his way home from work.
Johnson tried to slam the door in his face. "No use talking to
me," he said. "I'm finished with your advice." But Bush
Lawyer Bloggs would advise what not to do as quick as he'd
advise what to do. And he was dead set against Johnson going
to Europe. Said the furthest he'd been from Footscray was to
the Werribee racecourse, so he'd only make a fool of himself
in Europe. "There's enough idiot Australians running
around Europe boasting about Phar Lap and Australian beer,
without you joining in," he told What Do You Reckon. Johnson told him he was going to Europe whether he liked it or
not. "Don't blame me if you end up in an aeroplane crash or
get poisoned eating frogs' legs in France or get clobbered in
London for calling the Duke a Pommy bastard." But old
What Do You Reckon was determined to tempt fate. "Never
thought I'd live to see the day when my best friend would

decide to go to Europe—against my advice and considered opinion," the bush lawyer said, and then started to advise him about the best travel arrangements.'

'This story better have a good ending. Have another drink and get to the point.'

' "It's too late," says What Do You Reckon Johnson, backing away. "I've finalised all arrangements." Bush Lawyer Bloggs was ropeable. "What airline are you travelling on?" "Qantas." "What? The worst service in the world—drack sorts for hostesses, poor service, drunken pilots. Change your ticket to BOAC." Then he asks What Do You Reckon which pub he has booked into in London. When he hears, he performs again. "Worst pub in London. Bugs in the beds, the lifts don't work, crook tucker, and the waiters won't talk to you under a two dollar tip." '

'Did What Do You Reckon change his itinerary?'

'No, he told the bush lawyer to mind his own business, which is about the biggest insult you can offer any lawyer, bush or otherwise; they're all tarred with the same brush. "That's what I call gratitude," Bush Lawyer Bloggs harped on. "I've advised you, man and boy, for thirty years and never put you on the wrong track once, and me a man who's travelled the world three times and willing to let you have the benefit of my experience free of charge, without fee or favour." '

'When the bush lawyer found out his mate was going to the English Derby, he gives him a tip. "I've already got a tip. Right from Scobie Breasley himself," old What Do You Reckon says. "He's going to ride the winner again this year." Bush Lawyer Bloggs really got upset this time. "What? Breasley's old enough to be on the pension. He couldn't ride the winner of the Darwin Cup, let alone the Derby." But What Do You Reckon wouldn't listen, and when he was due to leave, he called at the shop to say goodbye and delivered the final blow to Bush Lawyer Bloggs' ego. He says he's going to Rome for an audience with the Pope. "Now I've heard everything. You? A mug like you, a disgrace to the Church, to get an audience with the Pope! Be your age. Think you can just walk into the Vatican and get an audience with the Pope? Listen, mate, if you'd told me earlier I could have arranged it, but now you've got no hope."

'The bush lawyer was heart-broken, but he put a fatherly hand on What Do You Reckon's shoulder: "You've done the wrong things. It's sure as eggs you'll have a shocking air trip; you'll be uncomfortable at the pub; Breasley won't win the Derby and you won't get an audience with the Pope. But I'm not a man to bear grudges. Just to show there's no hard feeling, I'll give you a free haircut to keep you going until you get back. At least, you'll look the part while you're making a fool of yourself." '

'How did What Do You Reckon get on overseas?'

'Well, he leaves with a nice new haircut and the bush lawyer sees him off at the airport. "If you need any advice, just send an air letter and I'll cable my reply." Well, the bush lawyer gets a card after a few days: "Wonderful trip. Qantas the best air service in world." Then a few days later: "Best pub in England, good beer, good tucker, air-conditioned lifts and no tips allowed." Next thing he gets a cable: "Breasley won the Derby on a ten-to-one shot."

'The poor old bush lawyer was so upset he stopped giving his customers advice for a week. He hears no more until one day What Do You Reckon walks into the shop, large as life and grinning from ear to ear. The first thing the bush lawyer said was: "Bet you didn't get an audience with the Pope." "Yes, I did." "Well, you must have mentioned my name," the bush lawyer says. "I didn't mention your name," Johnson replies. "I gets in there and kneels and kisses the ring on the Pope's finger." The bush lawyer can't wait. "And what did the Pope say to you?"

'Old What Do You Reckon walks to the shop door ready to run. "He gives me his blessings and he says —" "What did he say?" the bush lawyer asks. And What Do You Reckon replies: "The Pope says to me as I'm kneeling there: 'My son, where on earth did you get that haircut?' " '

'You're getting worse; a bigger liar than Tom Pepper.'

34

That Australians love to be praised.

AUSTRALIANS ARE THE MOST WONDERFUL PEOPLE IN ALL THE WORLD

There I was in the Harold Park Hotel watching TV when Truthful Jones walked in.

'Watching the television ads again,' he said with a sly grin.

'Was watching *The Hendersons*,' I defended. 'My son, Alan, produced it . . .'

Truthful threw a hundred-dollar note on the counter. 'The TV ads are better than the programs; more money spent on making them. Drink that down and have another.'

'What, you won the Lotto or something?' I said, in shock.

'Got the trifecta on the first race at the dogs, across the road—and decided to quit while I was in front.'

Just at that moment, a singing commercial came on. 'I'm my own man and my own boss . . . Australian in my soul and breast.'

Truthful commented, 'Gees, those ad men are cunning; every second ad praises Australia: "I love Cornflakes—and Australia"; they work on the old Australian inferiority complex. The Yanks know how to handle that complex. "What do you think of Australia?" a journo asks. The Yank replies:

"The most wonderful country in the world"—and that's before he leaves the airport.'

I ventured, 'Australia's a great country being ruined by big business and small-minded politicians.'

Truthful took to the theme. 'Yeh, here's your beer. It's the biggest con in history: the lucky country . . .'

I replied: 'But it's aimed at hiding the fact that the country's stuffed; and capitalism is in the middle of a depression everywhere.'

'Spot on,' Truthful warmed up. 'Big business kids the people that it's patriotic, whereas they're all multinationals.'

Truthful had me: it's one of my favourite themes. 'Did you know,' I asked, 'that the sponsor for the Australian of the Year is Mitsubishi, a Japanese based multinational?'

'No, but I do know that this patriotism is a Bandaid to cover the wounds of the poor. Met a bloke sleeping on a park bench—and he said: "Australia's a great country, mate . . ." '

'He must have seen the ads on TV in a shop window,' I said. 'It's a con, all right, and not only in Australia. The Yanks run "Buy American" campaigns while we run "Buy Australian". There'd be an end to world trade if the plans succeeded. Did I ever tell you my theory that the world is run by multinationals, and each government manages the economy for them, like Hawke and Keating? Patriotism is the last refuge of a scoundrel, as Doctor Johnson once said . . .'

Truthful asked, 'Did I ever tell you about the Irish migrant who went back to Dublin?'

'No, I don't think you did. Have a drink and tell me about him. Australians complain that some migrants who go back to the old country haven't got a good word to say for Australia . . . the inferiority complex again.'

'Well, this particular Irishman was different. When he arrived back in Dublin after five years his mate said to him: "And how was it, Pat, old mate, what koind of people are these Aussies after all?" "The Australians?" says Pat. [Truthful affected a passable Irish accent.] "Oi'm glad you asked that question. They're the most wonderful people in all the woide world. And that's the simple truth. With the Australians it's a case of share and share aloike, one for all and all

163

for one. It's what they call mateship. The stranger comes to them and they make him welcome, the loike of the prodigal son returning in the Bible, and him not a son at all nor any relative even. But the Australians will give him first place by the foire. And, Oi tell yer no loie, if you have no money and the Aussie has two dollars, he'll give you one and never ask for it back. Ah, they're darlin' people, the only true Christians left in the world. If you're a fugitive on the run, the Aussie will hoide you and keep you safe. No matter what you do, your Australian mate will defend you. 'A mate can do no wrong.' And no matter who you are, the Australian will give you a fair go." '

'Here's your beer. He was certainly wrapped up in Australians.'

'Was he ever.'

'And there's a lot in what he says.'

'You admit Aussies are good people, I see,' quipped Truthful. 'You know, Australians like to be praised. "What do you think of Australia?" That's the first thing they ask a foreign visitor. One time, a Sydney taxi-driver asked one of those visiting Yankee wrestlers: "What do you think of Sydney?" And the Yank replies: "I like it—and the thing I like most about it is there's a daily plane service, so I can get to hell out of this place and go back to God's own country." '

'Ah, these Yanks think there's no place like the USA. But this Irishman must have met some real nice people while he was here.'

'Must he ever. Wait till I tell you. So his mate says, "Pat," he says, "they must be marvellous people, the Australians, and no mistake." And Pat is just getting warmed up. "It's loike I'm tellin' yer, they're the most wonderful people in all the world. Let me take just another small example. You know how I loike a drop of the roight stuff. Well, more than once in Australia, Oi took one over the noine and woke up with a mother and a father of a hangover. But, when you've got a hangover the Aussie, may God bless his endeavours, would offer you a drink to loiven you up. What he calls the hair of the dog that bit you. Ah, they're darlin' boys, people after me own heart. Do you know, if you have no home the Australian

164

will invoite you in to live in his home. And if you have no bed, he'll let you have his bed. And, may God stroike me dead if I tell a loie, if you have no wife, the Australian will let you share his wife." '

'He could see nothing but good in Australians.'

'Well, his mate says to him, "Pat," he says, "oi'll admit from what you say Australians must be foine upstandin' people— but surely you found something in Australia you didn't loike?" Pat hesitates for a moment, rubs his chin and says thoughtfully: "Well, Oi will admit Oi didn't get on too well with the whoite people out there." '

35

That cricket, like grand opera, is funny because it is so deadly earnest.

THE BEST OPENING BAT IN QUEENSLAND

Truthful Jones is not a cricket fan so I must supply the cricket legend myself. With Fiery Fred Trueman, I published a book of forty-three yarns about cricket. I thought Fred and I had exhausted the funny side of cricket (which is funny because it's so deadly earnest—like grand opera—but then I heard this here yarn about a horse who played cricket).

Years ago, in Australia, there was a boom in pub cricket. The drinkers at one hotel would challenge the drinkers at another hotel to a friendly game. The publicans would supply two or three eighteen-gallon kegs of beer and a good time would be had by all.

Melbourne Cup Day was also a favourite occasion for pub cricket matches. In fact, this particular match which has gone down in history was actually played on Melbourne Cup Day, 1963, in a place called Boraloola. That day, the crowd got free beer, a free cricket match, a bet on the Cup—and they saw the eighth wonder of the world.

After a few grogs to see them go, the captains tossed and the revelry was about to begin.

The umpires were ready to go on to the field, each with a

jug of beer in hand to improve his vision so he could give decisions to his own team without fear or favour.

The star of the visiting team, an opening batsman, was also ready; he wore one batting glove (on the wrong hand); one of his pads was white, the other tan; his trousers were navy blue and he wore a tee-shirt labelled BEER IS A FOOD—and a digger's hat. His bat was split and repaired with string dipped in tar.

Two drunks, after a long struggle, had managed to peg down the matting on the asphalt wicket. They then proceeded to put the stumps in, discovered there were only five—and substituted a branch from a wattle tree with yellow blooms on top of it.

The game was about to proceed when the visiting captain did a slow head count to make sure his team were all present. Only ten men. He double checked. Only ten bloody men. He called on his team to line up. 'There's some bastard missing; it's Sammy Smith, one of our opening batsmen,' the captain said. 'Sammy's definitely not here.'

The visiting captain approached the Boraloola committee and politely sought a replacement. The Boraloola mob weren't keen to help out: they'd wagered heavily on the local team.

At last, an old bloke sitting in a cart under a nearby tree called to the visiting captain: 'Maybe I can help you, mate!'

The captain walked over, a trifle unsteadily, had a look at the old fellow: getting on for eighty, about a dollar's worth of clothes on, corks in his hat and as skinny as a flagpole—would weigh about five stone wringing wet in an army overcoat with housebricks in the pockets.

He'd be useless, the captain decided, and asked, his features suggesting sarcasm and a fondness for beer: 'Fancy yourself as a cricketer, do you, mate?'

'No,' the old bloke replied. 'Never played the game in me life—but my horse is the best opening bat in Queensland.'

'Is he now?' the captain said and, being half pissed and ready for a joke, asked the Boraloola mob if he could bring in a horse as a replacement for Sammy Smith.

Well, the citizens of Boraloola had a conference around the

167

kegs and agreed: better to have a horse than a ring-in bats-man, which they suspected the visitors might be ready to come at.

By this time, the old bloke had unyoked his horse and approached the assembled cricketers.

'Hang on a minute,' he said. 'There's a few conditions attached to this. My horse here is an opening bat, the best in all bloody Queensland, so he will insist on opening the innings and facing the bowling, taking the first over.'

So it was agreed.

'And another thing, he'll want four pads: can't risk him getting injured in a picnic game.'

Well, by this time everybody was laughing their heads off—especially the Boraloola team. But the laugh was on the other side of their faces when they tried to scrape up four pads for the horse. The teams had only five pads between them and, as the old bloke was adamant on the horse wearing four of them, the star opening batsman had to surrender his white pad and was left with the tan one—on his wrong leg.

Word went around the town that the eighth wonder of the world was about to be seen in Boraloola—a horse opening the innings in a cricket match on Melbourne Cup Day! So the crowd swelled until six more kegs of beer had to be sent for.

At last, the two openers went to the wicket, amid ribald cheers from the well-oiled throats of the spectators.

The horse took guard—and promptly hit the first ball straight out of the ground for six.

The Boraloola crowd couldn't believe their eyes, especially when the horse cover-drove the second ball for four—cracked the third and fourth balls for six, the fifth for four—and the last ball of the most expensive over ever bowled in Boraloola for another six.

The star opening batsman faced the second over. He was in form and wanted to get the bowling for himself, so he played down the line until the fifth ball when he called the horse for a single.

But the horse just stood there, leaning on his bat.

When he saw the horse was refusing to run, the star bats-man turned and ran back. He nearly got run out.

He scowled at the horse, placed the next ball for an easy single and called again—but the horse didn't move. The star bat went back again and threw himself flat to just scramble home.

He got up, dusted his clothes, went down the wicket to the horse and he said: 'Listen, why didn't you run?'

'Run!' the horse replied. 'If I could run I wouldn't be here playing in a pub cricket match with a mug like you, I'd be down at Flemington racing in the Melbourne bloody Cup.'

36

That the Jolly Swagman was the most Australian Australian.

THE MOST IMPORTANT MAN IN AUSTRALIA'S HISTORY

'It's a mystery to me,' Truthful Jones began in the Harold Park Hotel, 'why no-one is writing the biography of Sam Hoffmeister . . .'

'Sam who?' I asked.

'Sam Hoffmeister . . .'

'Never heard of him. What was he, a South Australian wine grower?'

'No, he was a Bavarian anarchist.'

'You don't tell.'

'Positive fact. My grandfather knew Sam, knew him well, fought with him in two shearers' strikes back in the nineties in Queensland . . .'

'You'd better have another drink and tell me about him,' I said. 'And try pulling the other leg. What the hell would a Bavarian anarchist be doing shearing sheep?'

'The old Sam wasn't really a shearer, took up shearing in order to pursue his avocation as an anarchist, believed in the rule of Bryant and May . . .'

'And what is the rule of Bryant and May?'

Truthful picked up the box of matches from the top of his

cigarette packet on the bar. 'Who makes them?'

'Bryant and May used to,' I said, 'but why should Sam what's-his-name want them to rule?'

'Stands to reason. You know about the shearers' strike of 1891; you wrote about it in your play on Henry Lawson. Well, my grandfather and Sam Hoffmeister took part in that strike—and the other big strike of 1894.'

'But why should anyone write Sam's biography?'

'It's the bicentennial, right? And Sam Hoffmeister was the most Australian of all the Australians, more Australian than you or Paul Hogan, or any other half-shrewd mug.'

'How could a Bavarian anarchist be the most Australian Australian?'

'Well, Henry Lawson was the son of a Norwegian seaman and a woman of gypsy stock and you reckon he's our great national poet; well, Sam Hoffmeister was one of the men who set up the military camp at Barcaldine in 1891; you researched it for your play . . .'

'Yeh, but I didn't read about any Sam Hoffmeister . . .'

'You didn't do your homework properly. The old Sam preached that anarchism meant communal co-operative living without a central government, groups of republics.' Truthful tilted his hat back. 'How does it go again? "From each according to his ability and to each according to his needs." It was the strongest political movement in Australia in 1891, my grandfather reckoned; but the old Sam still had the co-operative republic in his skull right up until 1894. There was this squatter named MacPherson who hired scab labour, instead of union shearers. So they burned his shed down; or, rather, Sam Hoffmeister did . . .'

'The rule of Bryant and May,' I twigged.

'Twenty shearers, including my grandfather, rode to the Dagworth woolshed one Sunday night. On guard was a copper named Daly; he was armed with a carbine; MacPherson and his staff were also armed. The shearers fired a volley. My grandfather yelled: "Come out, you bastards, with your hands up or you'll die!" Daly and MacPherson fired shots into the night; but it was all a blind, to cover Sam Hoffmeister while he burned down the shed full of sheep. "Give it to the

171

bastards, boys, we've waited four years for this," Sam yelled, then he snuck to the woolshed with kerosene and a box of Bryant and May; then the shearers and Sam made good their escape. As luck would have it, heavy rain fell overnight and Squatter MacPherson and Constable Daly could find no tracks in the morning. The fire was written up in the southern press which said it was a part of a plot to set up an anarchist republic in western Queensland, which was true. Anyway. MacPherson and Constable Daly rode to Winton and enlisted the aid of two more troopers, named Cafferty and Dyer. Meanwhile, back at their camp by the Diamantina River, Sam and his mates ate mutton and damper. Well, eventually, Mac-Pherson, the squatter, mounted on his thoroughbred, and the three troopers found Sam Hoffmeister and his mates camped by the billabong . . . and so "Waltzing Matilda" was born.'

'What the hell has all this got to do with "Waltzing Matilda"?' I interjected.

'A lot. It was Sam Hoffmeister who introduced the term into Australia; when the other shearers said they were "humping Bluey" (carrying a swag), Sam would say, "I'm awltzing with Mathilde." Y'see, Mathilde was a name given by German soldiers to their camp followers, hundreds of years ago. Later, when prostitutes weren't allowed to travel with armies, they called their overcoats Mathilde. In the First World War they were amazed when they heard Australian soldiers singing "Waltzing Matilda", when they themselves had a similar song (a'course they'd never heard of Sam Hoff-meister—and neither had the Australian soldiers . . .).'

'And neither had I until you started to tell this unbelievable story . . .'

Truthful wasn't happy. 'What? So that's all the thanks I get . . . Anyway, Sam Hoffmeister had been saying [here Truthful quoted in halting German]: "auf der walz mit Mathilde" for four years since the big battles at Barcaldine. And the idea of saying awltzing with Matilda caught on, all over Queensland; my grandfather wrote a poem about old Sam.'

'How did it go?' I asked, suspending disbelief just for a minute.

'Well, the night after the fire, Sam's mates saw him burn

172

some papers in the campfire. Some of the shearers said he'd burned a letter that had come on the mail coach a few days before from Brisbane, giving him the nod that scabs would work the Dagworth shed; but my grandfather reckoned Sam had told him the papers were a detailed plan to set up an anarchist republic in western Queensland.'

'But . . .' I tried to interject.

'There's no buts: I've got a dog race to catch across the road—and I'm givin' you the greatest idea since *Power Without Glory*.'

Truthful began to sing through his nose:

'Up rode the squatter mounted on his thoroughbred
Up rode the troopers, one, two, three!
And they soon searched the camp and found Winchester rifles . . .'

Mercifully he stopped singing. 'They also found revolver cartridges, plus gelignite. The cartridges matched the ones found near the Dagworth shed after the battle. All the boys denied anyone had left the camp. "What's that you've got in your tucker bag?" Squatter MacPherson asked Sam Hoffmeister. "Where are those papers that came to you in the Brisbane mail the other day?" And do you know what Sam replied?'

I leaned my head in my arms on the bar and muttered: 'You'll never take me alive . . .'

'Spot on! And do you know what happened then?'

'He jumped into the billabong . . . this is ridiculous!'

'Ridiculous nothing, and he didn't jump into the billabong; he shot himself!'

'I believe you, Truthful, but thousands wouldn't. But pray tell where Banjo Paterson comes into all this?'

'Banjo arrived at the Dagworth station the year after Sam Hoffmeister died—as a guest of Squatter MacPherson. (Banjo was courting a sheila in the district, name of Sarah.) MacPherson told Banjo about the attack on the woolshed and recited a rough version of the poem, "Awaltzing mit Mathilde". Banjo had never heard of the term "waltzing Matilda", him being a New South Welshman, where it was unknown, but he got the idea of adapting the poem when he heard a lady guest playing on the harpsichord a tune she'd heard played by a German band at the Warrnambool races . . .'

'But the tune of "Waltzing Matilda" is the same as an English song "Once a Jolly Soldier".

'Be that as it may, Banjo heard the tune and adapted the poem which became the song "Waltzing Matilda". A'course, being a squatter's friend, he toned it down, had it that Sam was wanted for stealing a sheep, whereas he was to be charged with arson, conspiracy and sedition; did you ever hear of three troopers and a squatter being needed to arrest a man for stealing one sheep? And he had Sam jump into the billabong . . .'

'And may I ask just once more: how did the original go?'

Truthful took off his hat and scratched his napper. 'Well . . . let's see . . .' He began to sing in a bush through-the-nose chant:

'Once the old Sam Hoffmeister camped by a billabong
Under the shade of a coolibah tree,
And he sang as he watched his old billy boiling
"auf der walz mit Mathilde . . ." '

I objected in sheer frustration: 'Shut up, Truthful!' but Truthful would not relent.

'Awaltzing Matilda and hiding a tuckerbag
Who'll come awaltzing Matilda with me?'

Truthful ordered a drink and continued: 'I forget the next verse but . . .'

'Down came the squatter mounted on his thoroughbred
Down came the troopers, one, two, three!
Where's that anarchist propaganda you've got in your
tuckerbag?
You'll come awaltzing Matilda with me!
But old Sam he up and grabbed hold of his rifle
"You'll never take me alive," said he.
And his ghost may be heard as he sings by the billabong
"auf der walz mit Mathilde . . . with me".'

'Truthful,' I vowed, 'one of these days, I'm going to murder you in the middle of one of your stories. So help me God, I'll hang for you yet!'

Truthful grinned enigmatically. 'Well, that's not word for word—but one thing is for certain: Banjo censored it. For instance, he took out Sam's name and the mention of the plan for the anarchist republic . . .'

'There was such a plan in 1891,' I said, 'and I never heard of it being connected with "Waltzing Matilda" . . .'

'Ah, the old Sam Hoffmeister was in that move up to his neck; was a mate of William Lane. Billy buzzed off to Paraguay and formed the republic there, but the old Sam was a stubborn Bavarian and he stuck with the anarchists who refused to go with Lane. And old Sam was on the way to have another crack at it in Queensland when he met his untimely end . . . You should write a book about him, the greatest Australian of them all . . .'

Truthful took himself across the road to the Harold Park dog track.

I didn't believe a word of his story; but just in case I did some research in the Mitchell Library and had a mate check the Queensland Law Reports for 1894.

And would you believe? An inquest was held into the death of one Samuel Hoffmeister, who shot himself by the Four Mile Billabong near Kynuna, Queensland. The Dagworth woolshed fire was mentioned at the inquest, but the arrested shearers stuck to their alibi and no charges were laid. It was suggested that Hoffmeister might have received a bullet wound in the Dagworth fire battle.

37

That the halt, the lame and the dead vote early and often in Australian politics

THE WIZARD OF OZ

Once upon a time in the great south land of Oz, there lived a wizard. He had much fame in the land as a counter of heads and pieces of paper.

His counting was usually done in secret, yet the wisest people in the land knew what he did.

His greatest achievement as a counter of paper became the best-kept secret in the history of the land of Oz.

It was the time of Pass-off when the representatives of the people passed themselves off as servants of the citizens of Oz, instead of pharisees and philistines.

When the time of Pass-off came around again, like the Palsy, of which the citizens of Oz were very sick, they conducted freely a ritual known as the Ballot: each citizen of one score years and six and over, received a piece of paper known as a vote.

Citizens, in secret, each made a choice and placed their votes in a ballot box. At the end of the day the pieces of paper were counted and, by this quaint means, it was decided who should rule over the land of Oz for three years: Labor-dee or Liber-dum.

The Wizard of Oz was the chief numbers man for Labor-dee.

As the day of the ballot approached, the Wizard became sad at heart, for being skilled in the ways of numbers and pieces of paper, he saw in a vision that Labor-dee might have less pieces of paper than Liber-dum when the ballot was counted.

Behold, at that time the King of Oz was full of pride, and confident he would be elected king for the third time.

But the Wizard came to him and spake thus: 'I fear we shall have less pieces of paper than Liber-dum; we'll get done like a last supper.'

'Ah, ye of little faith,' saith the king. 'The thin books and the idiot screens say we will have the most papers.'

'They may be wrong,' quoth the Wizard. 'Much hunger stalks the land, and homeless children wander the streets of all the cities and towns.'

So the King of Oz summoned his servants who controlled the thin books and idiot screens and he spoke to them saying: 'Give me the most pieces of paper and there will be tidings of great joy. In three years not one child in the land of Oz shall be hungry or homeless, and there shall be no more crying, neither shall there be any more pain.'

But the people believed him not—there were murmurings in the land that the rich grew richer and the poor poorer, that it mattered not who had the most papers, for were not the Liber-dums also servants of the rich?

Nevertheless, most of the people of Oz were dutiful, and those who did not mark the paper were obliged to pay 100 shekels (known then as dollars).

Next, the Wizard spake to the Apostle of the Money Changers in the Temples of Oz saying: 'The King listens not, yet the infidels of Liber-dum may have more pieces of paper.'

'Don't be a scumbag!' replieth the Apostle. 'To hell with the papers, so long as we have an abundance of seats.'

So quaint were the customs of Oz that the representatives of the people stood for seats. In each seat were many thousands of voters and their papers elected but one representative.

The Apostle replied: 'Verily, I say unto to you: no problems, for there are many in the land who will cast not their vote and you know the ways of casting votes for such people.'

The Wizard thought, 'this man is wiser than the king,' and he spake thus: 'Some of those who do not vote shall vote? Yes! And the lame and the dead shall also vote, though they never leave their sick beds or their graves.'

'Spot on, dick-head,' replieth St Paul. 'But only in the seats where we may lose, numbering scarcely more than twenty, and seek ye the help of Ray of Sunshine, of numbers.'

And so it came to pass that the people cast their votes save one in 20, who cared not who ruled the land of Oz. Those who lived in seats where vast numbers voted Labor-dee voted, knowing their papers were of no account, just as those who lived in seats where Liber-dum were sure to win did likewise. In these seats, the papers of those who did not vote remained unused—honesty ruled the affairs of the ballot.

But in 22 seats, the people who voted Labor-dee and Liber-dum were almost equal in number and here strange events came to pass. Voting ceased when the sun sank in the East (for all things were strange in the land of Oz), but in the hour before sunset, many men known as scrutineers, and a few other men called electoral officers did speak in divers tongues; and so procured the pieces of paper of the recently dead, the mortally sick, even for some people from foreign lands not yet registered to vote.

Pieces of paper were placed in the ballot boxes and names crossed from the list of voters, and all these papers were marked for Labor-dee.

And the Apostle spake thus on the telephone to The Wizard of Oz: 'Did you and the Wizard Kid put in enough bodgie votes to swing those swinging seats?'

'No problems,' replied the Wizard. 'Ray will be at the official counting house when the numbers are counted on the idiot screen.'

'Tell him to hold his long tongue, else the Liber-dum mob twig to the trick.'

The multitude of all the nation of Oz watched the idiot screens all over the land as the votes were counted by computers, and a table of experts analysed the figures. Of all the voting experts in the land of Oz, one was by far the greatest and his name was called McKerosene. So skilled was he at analysis, that only one-and-half hours after sundown, he did declare: 'There has been a nationwide swing of two per cent to Liber-dum and I do hereby declare that Labor-dee has been defeated and the King deposed. So be it.'

But Ray, in the crude language of Sunshine, replieth, saying: 'Pigs arse. The swing of two per cent over the nation may not apply in the 22 swinging seats.'

And the experts laughed at him, saying: 'The machine cannot lie.'

But as the night wore on, they laughed on the other side of their faces, for the swing in the swinging seats went to Labor-dee. And so the last became first and the first last; and the King of Oz rejoiced and thanked God and the citizens of Oz.

Now, at that time, in the land of Oz, was a custom called talk-back radio which gave the citizens of Oz their only chance to talk back. And behold, on the first day of the week after the ballot, many citizens rang the talk-back to say that when they went to vote with their piece of paper they found that their names had already been struck off the list of voters, and these people dwelt in the swinging seats.

But soon the talk-back men, save one, ceased to listen to the swinging voters whose pieces of paper were thus misused and the Pass-off ballot was soon forgotten and nothing changed.

There dwelt in Oz at this time a scribe who had long ago written that the Labor-dee numbers men had often voted for the halt, the lame, the dead and the absent. And he spoke to the courageous talk-back man who gave him names of the voters whose pieces of paper had been stolen. And the scribe did search in all the swinging seats for signs and portents of evil.

And it was known in the land that this scribe was a hard man, though soft in the head many believed. And it came to pass that not all the Labor-dee men he had known in his youth had yet gone to the land of nod, and one of them did speak to him secretly saying: 'It is the Sugar Roberts factor brought back to life by the Wizard of Oz.' And he did in detail reveal to the hard scribe exactly how the result of the ballot was reversed. For the scribe, the mention of Sugar Roberts factor meant that the lame, the dead and the absent would 'vote often and late.'

So the soft-headed scribe pieced together the story of how Labor-dee won and, in the fullness of time, he took the story to the men who owned the thin books of Oz who numbered but three, although hundreds of these influential books existed.

At first, the scribes employed by the thin books were much intrigued by the scribe's story about the Wizard of Oz, and they placed it before their employers.

Now, where once the thin book men were supporters of Liber-dum, they had become supporters of Labor-dee because of the policies of the king and the Apostle, who had brought the Money Changers back into the Temples of Oz.

And so owners of all the thin books did meet and one of them saith unto his colleagues: 'It matters little to us who wins any election, so we should publish this story to the multitude, and huge will be the sales of thin books.'

And his colleagues did applaud his wisdom, until one of their number, who still owned thin books in Oz though no longer a citizen, spake: 'The right to use their piece of paper each three years keeps the citizens of Oz quiescent; if we allow this soft-headed scribe tell them the story of the lame, the dead and the absent voting, they will lose faith and remember again the hungry and homeless amongst them. I say we should never utter one word of this story.'

And they didn't.

The scribe was like a voice crying out in the wilderness.

And the citizens of Oz lived happily ever after—except the six hundred thousand who were fined 100 shekels for not using their pieces of paper.

Especially unhappy were the thousands of voters in the swinging seats whose pieces of paper had been used by the Wizard of Oz and the Wizard Kid, to vote for Labor-dee when most of them intended to vote for Liber-dum; or were very ill or very dead or very late or had no intention of voting at all.

But such things were of little account in the great south land of Oz, for the vast majority of its citizens knew, deep in their hearts, that it mattered not one tittle who should rule over them.

Then, in the fullness of time, spake the Chief Counter of all the papers of the Pass-off ballot in the land of Oz, and he said: 'The result is thrown into doubt. There were substantial defects in the voting figures for the ballot, between the number of papers issued and those returned.'

The thin books did not publish news of what the Chief Counter had reported.

But verily there lived in the land of Oz a man called Rollicking Robbo, whose work it was to read the late night news. This he did treat as funny bedtime stories. And he told the story of the ballot with a sly smile.

The people believed him not.

And it came to pass that the story of how Labor-dee defeated Liber-dum became as a fairy tale to be told to the children of Oz in future times.

The infidels of Liber-dum complained not at all. Instead they spoke amongst themselves: 'If the people of Oz were to lose faith in the Pass-off ballot, all would be lost.' And forsooth, they vowed secretly to become as clever as the Wizard of Oz.